"If he comes back, I'll fight for you. You'll fight for you. Between the two of us, we should be able to keep you safe."

"Who's going to keep *you* safe?" Lark asked.

"I'm pretty good at doing that myself," Cyrus said, taking her arm and leading her around the side of the building.

"I'm pretty good at doing it, too, Cyrus," Lark said as she lowered herself into the passenger seat of the car. "But even people who are good at taking care of themselves, people who have always kept themselves safe, need help sometimes. I learned that while I was lying in that trailer praying that God would send someone to help me. I'm not going to forget that you were the one He sent. And, if you're ever in trouble, if you're ever at the point where you really do need someone to step in, I can guarantee you that I'll be the first to show up."

She closed the door before he could respond.

It was for the best. Cyrus wasn't sure what he would have said.

Aside from her faith and her family, there's not much **Shirlee McCoy** enjoys more than a good book! When she's not teaching or chauffeuring her five kids, she can usually be found plotting her next Love Inspired Suspense story or wandering around the beautiful Inland Northwest in search of inspiration. Shirlee loves to hear from readers. If you have time, drop her a line at shirlee@shirleemccoy.com.

Books by Shirlee McCoy

Love Inspired Suspense

Mission: Rescue

Protective Instincts
Her Christmas Guardian
Exit Strategy

Capitol K-9 Unit

Protection Detail

Heroes for Hire

Running for Cover
Running Scared
Running Blind
Lone Defender
Private Eye Protector
Undercover Bodyguard
Navy SEAL Rescuer
Fugitive
Defender for Hire

Visit the Author Profile page at Harlequin.com for more titles.

EXIT STRATEGY

SHIRLEE McCOY

HARLEQUIN® LOVE INSPIRED® SUSPENSE

ISBN-13: 978-0-373-67684-2

Exit Strategy

This edition published by arrangement with Love Inspired Books.

www.Harlequin.com

Printed in U.S.A.

Therefore judge nothing before the appointed time;
wait until the Lord comes. He will bring to light what is
hidden in darkness and will expose the motives of the
heart. At that time each will receive their praise from God.

—*1 Corinthians* 4:5

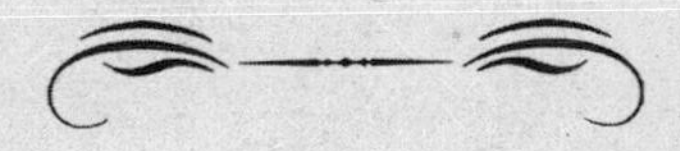

To Ronda Tumberg, who has always spelled my name correctly.

In loving memory of her sweet son Radley Eaton, who lived the entirety of his life in just a few short days, but who touched more hearts in that time than most people ever will.

ONE

Cold.

It speared through Lark Porter's long-sleeved sweater, settled deep into her bones. She shivered, clenching her teeth to keep them from chattering. The slivers of light that seeped through the cracks in the trailer during the day had disappeared hours ago. She'd waited, because she'd wanted Elijah Clayton's security team to think she had given up. She hadn't.

She wouldn't. Not now. Not in another day or two or three. Joshua deserved better than what he'd gotten. He deserved justice. She'd come to Amos Way to get it for him. She wouldn't quit before she accomplished that goal.

An image of her husband flashed through her mind. The way he'd been on their wedding day, happy and smiling, his dark suit just a little big in the shoulders. Joshua had written his own vows, promising to cherish Lark's heart for as long as they both lived.

Three years.

That was all they'd had.

Elijah's doing, and she planned to prove it.

Or die trying.

She rolled to her side, turning her back to the security camera and shimmying forward until her hands were level with the nail that stuck out of the wall. At least she'd been tied up with her hands in front of her. Every night, she tried to cut through the ropes that held her wrists. Every night, she failed.

Tonight might be different.

She held on to that thought, clung to it as she rubbed the rope against the nail. Back and forth. Up and down. Subtle movements. Slow movements. Counting. One. Two. Three. Wait ten. Start again. One. Two. Three. She missed and the nail raked against skin already raw from five nights' worth of struggling.

Five nights.

Six days.

Heading into another long night.

How many more did she have?

At some point, Elijah would be done with whatever game he was playing. When that happened, she would die. She knew that as surely as she knew that Joshua hadn't accidentally shot himself eighteen months ago, that he'd been murdered.

She dragged the rope against the nail again and again and again, thought the bonds might be loosening. Prayed that they were. As determined as she was, as much as she wanted to succeed, the odds were against her. She was tied up in a rotting trailer, sitting at the edge of a religious compound deep in the heart of a Pennsylvania forest. She could scream all she wanted, beg all she wanted, but there wasn't a person in the compound who'd help her. They all believed the lies, supported the cause. And the cause was Elijah's dogma, his doctrine.

Her stomach churned, the sickening scent of vomit and death filling her nose as she struggled to cut through the ropes. The dinner that had been left on a tray near the door only added to the awful stench. She'd made the mistake of eating meals three times. She'd lost hours after each one, drugged into a deep sleep that had left her disoriented, dehydrated and muddleheaded.

She couldn't afford to have that happen again. Now she didn't eat. She just smelled the rich aroma of stew and home baked bread. Prisoners in Amos Way were fed well.

And then, they died.

Accidental deaths.

Deaths that no one questioned, because no one in the community questioned anything.

There were rules and bylaws and community mores every member of the group agreed to. Even she and Joshua had, signing the contract that bound them to Amos Way for five years. They'd made it through three, and then Joshua had died, and Lark had left. She should have stayed away. It would have been the safe thing to do, the wise thing. But she'd had to know, she'd had to find out the truth. Joshua deserved that.

She missed the rope again. This time, the nail dug in so deep, blood slid down her arm. She wiped it against her skirt and kept working. One. Two. The rope shifted, the threads separating, blood rushing into her fingers.

Not free yet, but she could feel the ropes giving. She allowed herself a moment of celebration, a second of rejoicing. Maybe she could free herself. Maybe she could find her way out of the trailer, out of the compound, back to civilization.

If John McDermott and his security team didn't catch her before then. John had trussed her up so tight, she'd lost feeling in her feet and in her hands. Aside from the gouge she'd just cut in her arm, there were other signs that she'd been held captive. If she died, those marks would have to be explained. Or maybe not.

Maybe John would carry her body into the

woods, bury her deep enough that animals would never dig her up. She shuddered, tugging frantically against the rope. It gave, the sudden slack in it so surprising, she stilled.

Free?

It didn't seem possible, but she tugged again and the rope gave even more. Her pulse jumped, and she yanked one more time, the ropes giving completely. She didn't sit up, didn't reach down to free her ankles. She couldn't let the security team know she was free. If she did, they'd tie her up again, remove the nail, take away her one hope that she might actually get out of Amos Way alive.

She kept her arms in front of her, clutching the rope in her hand as she staggered to her knees, shuffled to the bathroom, her body so weak, she wasn't sure she'd make it.

There. Finally. No door to the room, but the camera was angled away, the bathroom tiny and windowless, offering no hope of escape.

She'd find another way out after she removed the rope from her ankles. It took too long, her muscles weak, her fingers still numb from too many days without good blood flow. Somewhere outside, a dog barked, the sound muted by the trailer walls. Was the security team heading her way? Had she been in the bathroom too long? Were they coming to check on her?

The thought made her heart beat faster, made her fingers even clumsier. The dog barked gain, the sound seeming to come from the other side of the wall. She gave up her fight with the ropes, shuffled out of the bathroom, her long skirt catching on broken tiles and debris, her knees bruised and aching. She settled down on the floor again, her back to the door that she knew would fly open at any moment. Someone would walk in, look around.

Check the ropes?

Please, God, don't let that happen.

She prayed because it was what Josh would have done, prayed because she had nothing else. No *one* else. Prayed because through everything, through all the sorrow and the grief and the uncertainty, faith had been her one constant, her one truth. God knew. He understood. He wanted justice as much as she did.

So, why was she lying in a putrid trailer alone?

She should have been back at work over a month ago, should have reported to her fifth grade classroom the third week of August. Had anyone noticed her absence? Had they gone looking for her? No one had come to the compound. She knew that for sure.

Her eyes burned with tears. She wouldn't let them fall. She hated crying almost as much as she hated quitting. She'd been a fighter her entire life, and she'd keep fighting, because there was nothing else to do. No other way out of the situation she'd gotten herself into.

And, she *had* gotten herself into it.

She could have refused her in-laws' invitation to return to Amos Way. She could have ignored the doubts that had nagged at her since Joshua's death.

Could have. Should have. Would have.

A hundred regrets, but she couldn't do anything about them.

Keys jingled. The lock on the door turned. The door opened, cold crisp air filling the darkness. She didn't dare turn to look at the person entering. Didn't dare move. Barely dared to breathe.

Please just let him be getting the food.

Please let him go away.

Please...

A light flashed on the floor near her head, glanced over the wall, landed on the nail still stained with her blood. He saw it. She knew that he did. Saw the trail of red that stained the dingy floor, the glossy drops that proved how she'd been spending her time.

She clutched the ropes that she'd broken

through, her heart slamming against her ribs, her stomach sick with dread. She could have turned, faced the man as he approached, but she still wanted to hope and believe that he didn't know, that he hadn't seen the broken ends of the rope, the trail of blood.

The floor creaked, boots tapping against linoleum.

Fabric rustled, and she felt him. Right there. Inches away. John? He'd been one of Joshua's best friends. They'd grown up together. But friendship didn't mean much in Amos Way. All that mattered was the group cause, the combined beliefs, the value of community and the blind faith in Elijah Clayton. Elijah had named her the enemy. He'd set her up, accused her of theft, beaten her, tossed her in the trailer and left her to rot. No one in Amos Way would question that. No one would come to her aid.

She swallowed down bile, refusing to give in to panic.

Someone touched her shoulder, and she flinched.

"You've gotten yourself into a dangerous situation," a man said. She didn't know the voice. Not surprising. Most of the men on Elijah's security team were outsiders, hired hands who got paid well to protect Amos Way.

She didn't respond. Didn't know what she was expected to say.

"So," he continued, reaching for her hands, his fingers untangling the loose ends of the rope. "We're going to play this my way. Then maybe we can both get out of here alive. Okay?"

Surprised, she shifted, rolling onto her back, looking straight into a stranger's face. Moonlight filtered in through the open door, splashing across dark jeans and dusty boots, white dress shirt, gun holster. He looked like every other security officer she'd seen in the compound, his dark hair cropped close, his face hard.

"Who are you?" she asked, because he hadn't ignored her like every other security officer had.

"Someone who is here to help, but it's going to take me a little time to get you out of here." He pulled something from his gun belt, and her blood ran cold, his words flying away before they could register. Handcuffs. If he got those on her, she'd never escape. It was now or not at all. Fight and run or stay and die.

She lunged up, slamming her body into his with so much force they both toppled over. Feet still tied, she had no choice but to crawl over him, scramble for the door, for that cold crisp fall night.

He grabbed her ankle, dragged her back.

He was too strong or she was too weak. Too many days without food. Too much time trussed up like a Thanksgiving turkey. She fought anyway, scratching and clawing and bucking against his weight. He pinned her easily, hard body pressing hers into the ground, his hands surprisingly gentle on her forearms.

"Stop!" he commanded.

She didn't, because she could still feel the cold air, the chance of escape just a few feet away.

He pressed his forearm to her throat without even enough pressure to make her flinch.

"Stop," he said again, his voice calm. "John is watching. You want him to come give me a hand?"

She froze, her body shaking with fear and adrenaline.

"Good. Now, how about we try this again?"

He grabbed both her wrists, snapped the handcuff onto one. She bucked up, arm flailing as she tried to avoid the other cuff. He snapped it on easily, and she knew she was done. That any hope that she'd had of getting out of the compound alive was gone.

He lifted her wrists, flashing his light on the deep cut that still seeped blood.

"You're a mess," he murmured, letting her

arms drop onto her stomach, reaching across her body and using pliers to yank the nail from the wall. "But there's not a whole lot I can do about it yet."

The nail dropped onto the floor, and he reached over, his body covering hers for a split second, something dropping onto her knuckles, falling onto her stomach.

Surprised, she grabbed it, felt the cool metal of a key.

Her heart jumped, and she met his eyes.

He didn't give any indication that he knew what she held, just dropped the nail into his pocket and stood. "Essex sent me. He's been worried. Now, stop trying so hard, Lark. You're just making things harder on both of us."

He walked outside, closed the door, sealing her in with the putrid air, the pulsing darkness, the cold metal key pressing against her palm and just the tiniest glimmer of hope that she wasn't as alone as she'd thought.

So much for an easy mission.

Cyrus Mitchell pulled the bloody nail from his pocket and frowned. As far as he could tell, it was the only thing in the trailer that had a sharp edge on it. Lark must have been working at the ropes for hours, sawing through the hemp until she'd finally freed herself.

She had to have noticed the security camera, had to have known that she was being watched twenty-four hours a day. Maybe she'd been desperate enough not to care. Or sick enough not to be thinking clearly. Whatever the case, she'd been determined, and she'd succeeded.

He'd taken that away from her, and it didn't feel good.

The key was his way of apologizing. Essex's name the information she needed to keep her hope alive. It wouldn't get her out of the trailer, but maybe it would keep her from giving up.

Hope, he'd learned a long time ago, was a key factor in survival. Without it, there wasn't a whole lot of reason to keep going.

He locked the trailer, tucked the key into his pocket and headed back across the compound. Security cameras lined the fence, pointing in and out of Amos Way, tracking the movements of everyone who came or went. For a peaceful, God-loving community, they didn't seem all that trusting of their fellow man.

But, then, Cyrus hadn't expected them to be. On the surface, Amos Way was exactly what it claimed to be—a religious commune designed to give its members a home away from worldly corruption and materialistic excess. Underneath, they were something else. Something a lot darker and a lot more dangerous. Cyrus hadn't needed to enter the compound to know it. He'd just had to watch the comings and goings of the armed security force. He wasn't sure what the team was transporting in and out, but he didn't think it was truckloads of Bibles.

He jogged the last hundred yards to security headquarters. The squadron was housed in a ranch-style building that looked over the fifty-acre compound. Cyrus had spent the past six nights bunking with fifteen loudmouthed, brash kids who had more muscle than brains. John McDermott ran the place like a military unit, and he'd assured Cyrus that he'd be moved into "officer" housing once he made it through his probationary period.

Cyrus had no intention of being in Amos Way long enough for that to happen. In and out. That's what he'd promised his boss Chance Miller. Head of HEART, Chance hadn't been all that eager to let Cyrus enter Amos Way. Cyrus wasn't all that happy about it either. HEART specialized in rescuing hostages from the most difficult of situations. The team's mission was to reunite families, to bring closure to those waiting for the missing. Sometimes, though, they took cases like this—a missing person who might or might not be at risk.

Cyrus preferred overseas assignments. Work Stateside tended to get him into trouble. He owed Essex Randolph, though. The guy had saved his hide in Iraq, and Cyrus didn't forget things like that. Not ever. Essex had been worried about Lark. A teacher at the school where he worked, she hadn't shown up for the first day of school or for any day after. She'd emailed a resignation to the school board, contacted the principal to let him know she wouldn't be returning. Cyrus had read the emails. They seemed on the up and up. Essex wasn't convinced, though. Lark loved her job, and she hated Amos Way. There was no way she'd ever willingly stay there.

That had been Essex's opinion, but it wasn't enough for the police to open a case. It was enough for Cyrus. He'd convinced Chance to let him check things out. He'd assured him that the case would be simple. It was turning out to be anything but that. Too bad he'd been so confident. It wouldn't have been a bad thing to have some backup waiting nearby.

The door to security headquarters opened as Cyrus approached, and John stepped outside. Tall with a belly that hung over his belt, the guy had a thick blond beard and balding head that made him look more like a young Saint Nick than the head of a security team. He wasn't someone to be messed with, though, and Cyrus doubted he was easily fooled. He wouldn't like that the enemy had infiltrated his team, and that's what Cyrus was. An enemy to the cause. Whatever that might be.

"You got everything squared away?" John asked.

He knew the answer. There wasn't a doubt in Cyrus's mind that John had been glued to the security monitor, watching the interaction between his newest security team member and his prisoner.

"What do you think?" Cyrus asked, because that was his persona—Louis Morgan. Kicked out of the army for bucking authority, a loose cannon who lived by his own moral code. Loyal to whoever paid the most money.

"Answer the question," John barked.

"She's handcuffed. Don't know why you're bothering. Doubt she has more than a couple of days left." Cyrus shrugged like it didn't matter, like he didn't care that an injured woman was being held prisoner in the compound.

"You think she needs a doctor?"

"Not my business whether she does or not," Cyrus responded. "I'm paid to do what you tell me. I did it."

The answer must have pleased John. He smiled. Not an easy happy smile. The predatory smile of a killer. "You just keep that in mind, Louie. We'll both be happier that way."

He walked back inside, and Cyrus followed because it was expected. He was on night shift, working until dawn. It was his first all-nighter, and from what he gathered, it meant he was moving up in John's esteem. No reason why he wouldn't be. He'd done everything he'd been asked, and his cover story was faultless and foolproof. All the paperwork in order, all the background stuff put in place by HEART.

"What else do we have on the agenda for tonight?" he asked as he entered the building.

"We've got a shipment coming in at two." John glanced at his watch. "You're going to help unload."

Cyrus's pulse jumped. He'd witnessed a couple of deliveries being made, but he had no idea what was in any of the boxes that had been unloaded and locked into storage units at the edge of the compound. He'd asked and been told to mind his own business. He had, because he'd still been searching for Lark, and he hadn't wanted to get himself into trouble before he located her.

"You want me to run patrol while I'm waiting?" he asked, making sure to keep his expression neutral.

"I want you to go back to the trailer."

"The one with the woman in it?"

"What other one have we been discussing

tonight?" John responded as he walked into the monitor room. Seven computers. Seven security guards. None of the men looked all that excited to be watching the screens. The way Cyrus heard things, nothing much ever happened at Amos Way. People in the community followed the rules because they wanted to. They'd come to break free of temptation and sin, to aspire to the higher living that their leader preached. That had worked out well for Elijah. Whatever he'd started here in Amos Way, whatever secret he'd hired John and his team to protect, it had been safe for a long time.

Not any longer, though. Not if Cyrus had anything to do with it.

"I want you to go back here." John tapped the screen that showed the inside of the trailer. Lark lay exactly where Cyrus had left her, lying on her back, her hands on her stomach. Only someone who knew she was holding something would notice that one hand was fisted and the other was slack.

"Why?" he asked, and John frowned.

"You know what, Louie? I don't like questions. I like my men to wait for orders and to keep quiet until they get them."

"Then maybe you should talk a little faster," he responded and wasn't surprised when the bored kids watching the monitors glanced their way.

"Maybe you should watch your mouth," John snapped.

"Sorry."

John eyed him for a moment, then nodded. "Good. You need to learn the rules, and you need to follow them. That's the way things are here. Now," he said, tapping the screen again. "Back to our problem. The woman took something from Elijah. He wants it back. You want to earn your place on my team, you're going to get her to tell you where she hid it."

"You got rules of engagement?" he asked.

"Nah. Anything goes. Just make sure you get the information before two. We ship her out when the delivery comes in."

Ship her out?

Was that code word for *terminate*?

He didn't ask. Louis Morgan wouldn't care.

He nodded. "You got a place I can question her?"

"What's wrong with the trailer?"

"Too close to the community. I wouldn't want anyone to hear her scream."

John frowned. "I didn't say torture her. I said question her."

Maybe the guy had some morals. Maybe he

wasn't as far down the rung of humanity as Cyrus had thought. "You said no rules."

"One rule. Don't kill her. Two. Don't bring the community down on our heads. We're the good guys here, Louie. You gotta keep that in mind."

"That's exactly why I want to bring her where no one will hear our little exchange." He smiled. "You leave it to me, boss. I'll get it done." Happily, because this was the perfect opportunity to get Lark out of the trailer without having the entire security team come down on them both. That would be a good start to getting her out of the compound, but it would only be a start. The compound was almost as well guarded as Fort Knox.

John hesitated. Then nodded. "Do what you have to do to get Elijah's property back."

"What is it she took?"

"That's not something you need to know."

"I can't ask for it, if I don't know what it is."

John scowled, his fingers brushing the handle of his Glock. "You questioning my methods, Louie?"

"Just trying to get a handle on the mission," Cyrus responded.

"She'll know what it is. Get the information, and there's a good bonus in it for you."

"And a move from the common barracks?" he asked, because he figured John would expect him to.

"That, too."

"Then, I guess I'd better get started." He stalked from the house without looking back, walked back to the trailer. He'd spent the past few days studying the compound's layout, memorizing the location and angle of every security camera. There weren't many places that weren't under surveillance. The old church was one of them. It was also one of the only buildings that had a computer in it. If he could access that, he could hack into the mainframe that ran the security cameras, cut them off and get Lark out.

One thing at a time, Mitchell.

He could almost hear Stella Silverstone's voice. They'd been on more than one mission together, and she'd have accompanied him on this one if he hadn't been working for free. She'd offered to go with him anyway, but he didn't want to owe her. Not the way he owed Essex.

Not the way he owed Amber.

He shoved the thought away, refusing to think about the promise he made, the one he hadn't been able to fulfill.

He unlocked the trailer door, glanced over his shoulder and saw John slip behind an outbuilding.

The guy pretended to trust Cyrus, but he was suspicious. That would make things more difficult but not impossible. Never impossible.

Even in the worst of circumstances, a way out could be found. A good thing to keep in mind on a night like this.

TWO

Lark listened to the sound of footsteps on linoleum, her eyes squeezed shut, her grip tight on the key. She didn't dare turn to see who was coming. The key was her one hope of escape, and she was afraid whoever it was would see it and take it from her.

Beside her, fabric rustled and the floor creaked.

She didn't open her eyes. Let whoever it was think that she was asleep. Better yet, let him think she was unconscious. Maybe he'd go away. Leave her alone to figure out how she could open the cuffs without being seen by the security team.

"I know you're awake." The voice was smooth and rich, and she recognized it immediately. The man who'd dropped the key. The one who'd mentioned Essex.

Was it a trick? Some sort of mind game to get her to…

What?

Confess to searching Elijah's office?

She'd been caught doing that, so eliciting a confession wouldn't make any sense. But, then, nothing had made sense since she'd arrived back at Amos Way. Not her mother-in-law's silence. Not her father-in-law's fanaticism. Eric had changed since Joshua died. Not in a good way.

"Lark." The man sighed. "Let's not play games, okay? We're on borrowed time as it is." He cupped her biceps, pulled her up easily. She was sitting, then standing so quickly she felt dizzy with it. For a moment, she was back in time, standing with Joshua, looking at the compound for the first time, listening to him talk about growing up free from the trappings of the world, tuned into nature and focused on The Creator. She'd fallen in love with the picture he'd painted, but, then, she'd already been in love with him.

"You going to walk with your eyes closed or do you want me to carry you out of here? Either works for me."

The words were a splash of ice water in the face. She jerked away, the key pressed so hard into her palm, she knew the imprint of it would be left in her skin.

He didn't try to pull her back, just stood

where he was, blocking her path to the door. Maybe six-foot, a hundred and eighty pounds. Big compared to Lark, but she'd never been intimidated by physical strength. At least not in recent years. When she'd been a kid, walking home in one of the roughest neighborhoods in Chicago, she'd been scared. She'd gotten over that quickly. The will to survive and the knowledge that she only had herself to depend on had made her tough. The key to taking down a bigger, tougher opponent was the element of surprise. Without it, she didn't have a chance.

She lunged forward, aiming her foot for the man's instep and hitting her mark. He grunted, and she rammed both fists into his stomach, hopped out the door into the cold clean air. With her ankles tied, she couldn't move fast, but she stumbled down the stairs, managed to stay upright as she headed across overgrown grass. She didn't know where she was going, didn't have a clue as to where she could find safety. If she managed to escape the fenced area, she'd have to trek through thick forests to get to civilization. The closest town was a tiny speck on the map—seventy miles away, fifteen hundred people, ten full-time police officers. One of them with deep connections to Amos Way. She might not find allies there, but at least she could find a phone, could call a friend to give her a ride back to Baltimore.

The compound's main gates were to the north, but heading there wouldn't do her any good. She tried to run toward the side of the trailer, tripped on her feet and the ropes that bound her ankles. She fell hard, the breath knocked from her lungs, her fists slamming into her gut.

She tried to get to her feet.

"You don't know when to give up, do you?" the man asked, yanking her upright.

"I'll never give up," she replied, but her voice was weak, her body trembling.

"Great. Good. You just keep on fighting, but how about you don't fight me?" He moved her forward, nudging her toward the old church where she and Josh had gotten married. It stood on a hill overlooking the compound, its clapboard siding whitewashed and gleaming in the moonlight. Behind it, a small cemetery spread out across two acres. Just beyond that, the fence protected the members of Amos Way from intruders. Or kept them from leaving.

She didn't know why he was leading her there, and she dug her heels in, tried to stop their forward momentum. She stumbled, would have gone down if his arm hadn't wrapped around her waist.

"Keep moving," the man murmured, his fingers loose, his grip light. "Do you want John to join us?"

"I want to leave!" she responded, her voice raspy and hot sounding.

"You and me both," he replied, prying her hand open and taking the key from it.

She wanted to scream, cry, beg for mercy, but that was another thing she'd learned a long time ago—don't let your opponent see your fear.

"You want to go, then leave," she managed to say, and he shook his head.

"It would be nice if it were that easy, but John has this place sealed up tight. Getting out isn't going to be as easy as getting in, and even that wasn't all that easy." He lifted her wrists, used the key to unlock the handcuffs, pulled a knife from his gun belt.

Her mouth went dry, and she tried to back up.

"Calm down, Lark. I'm not planning to use this on you." He bent over, sliced through the ropes at her ankle.

Blood flooded into her feet. She didn't have time to think about it. He gave her a gentle push toward the church.

"Here's how we're going to play things. You're going to keep looking terrified—"

"Looking?" she mumbled, and he met her eyes, offered a half smile that did nothing to ease the hardness of his face.

"Just keep on *being* terrified. John wants me to question you about whatever it is you took from Elijah."

"I didn't take anything." She hadn't had a chance. She'd managed to sneak into Elijah's house during the evening prayer meeting, but she'd been caught before she could do more than open his file cabinet. Whatever he was hiding, whatever the compound fronted for, she hadn't had time to uncover it.

"That's not what John and Elijah think."

"I don't really care what they think."

"Maybe you should since they had you hog-tied in a trailer."

"And sent you to question me," she pointed out. "You probably know more about what they want then I do."

"Probably not. I've barely spoken to Elijah, and John keeps things close to the cuff."

"So you're just blindly following orders?"

"I'm helping a friend," he said, glancing over his shoulder and frowning. "Essex was worried about you. The police weren't listening to his concerns, so he asked me to check on you. I guess it's fortunate for you that he did."

She'd met Essex a year and a half ago, not

long after Joshua's death. She'd been substituting at the school where he taught fifth grade. At the end of the year, she'd been offered a contract to teach full-time. The job had been a godsend. So had Essex. He'd taken her under his wing, brought her home to meet his kids and wife. He was the closest thing to a family she had.

She'd hoped he'd worry when she didn't show up for work, but the first day of school had come and gone, and the police hadn't shown up, no one had come looking for her. She'd realized she was on her own, trapped because she'd been just foolish enough to think she'd be safe in a place that had killed her husband.

"How do you know Essex?" she asked, still not convinced this wasn't some kind of bizarre trick to get her to let her guard down, give in to whatever it was they had planned for her.

"We were army buddies."

That fit. Essex had retired from the military a few years before he'd become a teacher. "How many kids does he have?"

"Four."

"How old is he?"

"Do *you* know?"

"Yes."

"I don't. It's not something we discussed. I

can tell you this, though, he's got a scar on his forearm from saving my hide."

That fit, too. At least, the scar did. She didn't know about the life saving part. She'd asked about the scar, and Essex had simply said that he'd been injured while serving in Iraq. "What's his wife's name?"

"Janet. Kids are Essex Jr., Eleanor, Eliza and Elliot. Don't know what the *E* name thing is, but I told him he needs to cut it out," he growled. "Now, if you're done with twenty questions, how about we get down to business?"

"What business?"

"Getting out of here alive."

Whether he was telling the truth or a lie didn't matter. What mattered was that her arms were free, her feet were free. Soon the blood that pulsed back into her toes would calm, the throbbing pain would ebb and she'd have feeling back. That would make escape easier, and that was all she cared about. That and taking Elijah Clayton down. She might not have found evidence in his office, she might not have gotten her hands on something that could prove he was as dirty as the old hound dog he kept tied to a stake behind his house, but she knew he'd killed Joshua. Or had him killed.

Either way, Joshua's blood was on his hands.

She'd known it the day she'd found Joshua,

his hunting rifle in his hand, a bullet hole through his temple. She'd known Joshua. He was careful and cautious. He didn't take chances. The *accident* that had taken his life wouldn't have happened to someone like him. Couldn't have happened. The police had bought the lie, though. Why wouldn't they have? Even Joshua's parents had believed it.

Lark had been too numb to question what she was told.

She'd let her in-laws plan the funeral, let herself be led through days of grieving. When it was over, she'd packed up a few things, left the compound because it was too filled with memories of the only man she'd ever loved.

It had taken a couple of months for the truth to settle in, for the nagging disquiet to be replaced by the certainty that there was more to Joshua's death than a simple accident. She'd started digging, then, researching Amos Way, its history, its former members. There weren't many of those. The ones she'd found hadn't been willing to talk.

That hadn't stopped her.

She'd kept asking, thinking she was clever enough to stay a step ahead of Elijah. Obviously, she hadn't been.

She moved up the church stairs, the night dead silent, the compound still. Her in-laws were sleeping in their house, tucked safely away from whatever it was they'd run from. Life? Hardship? The world? Whatever it was, they'd been in Amos Way for nearly thirty years. They believed the lies, and they bought the status quo. They wanted what was best for the group, and they were willing to believe Lark was a thief, that she'd gone into the trailer willingly to commune with God and find the right path, rather than believe their leader wasn't who he pretended to be.

That hurt, but she couldn't think about it. Not when she finally had a chance at freedom. She knew the old church, the large sanctuary, the bell tower, the door that led into the cemetery. She knew how far she needed to go to make it to the fence. Joshua had taught her how to climb it. He'd taught her a lot of things. Mostly he'd taught her to love, to have faith, to believe that God had a perfect plan for all of their lives.

She wouldn't forget those lessons.

Not ever.

And, she wouldn't let his murderer go unpunished, wouldn't let his death be for nothing. Someone had to bring Elijah Clayton down. The way Lark saw things, it might as well be her.

The man opened the church door, and she stepped inside, the dry cool air filled with the musty scent of time and age. She'd loved this place, had felt more at home here than she'd ever been anywhere before, but it wasn't home anymore, and all she wanted was to escape. Maybe the man escorting her was Essex's friend. Maybe he wasn't. It didn't matter. She wasn't going to trust him to save her. She'd save herself.

He closed the door, sealed them inside the century old building. Then, he took her arm and led her through the empty sanctuary.

Lark didn't resist as Cyrus led her through the old church.

That surprised him.

He'd done his research before he'd approached John, and everything he'd learned about Lark had told him she was a leader, a go-getter, a survivor. Not that there'd been much to discover. Financial records only went back as far as her college days. She'd attended Towson University on scholarship, gotten a degree in elementary education. From what he'd been able to gather, she'd met her future husband there, moved into Amos Way after they'd married. Her husband had died of a self-inflicted gunshot wound nearly three years later. That's what the police report had said.

Essex didn't think Lark believed it.

That's why he'd been worried when she hadn't returned, why he'd contacted Cyrus and asked for help when the police couldn't step in. This was what HEART did best—entering areas the authorities couldn't or wouldn't go, finding the missing, bringing them home.

"Sit." He pressed her into the front pew and was surprised when she didn't fight him.

"Who are you?" she asked, her voice echoing hollowly in the empty building.

"To John and Elijah? Louis Morgan. Ex-military. Current mercenary. In other words, gun for hire."

"Who are you really?"

"Cyrus Mitchell. I work for HEART."

"Never heard of it."

"Most people haven't." He didn't have time to explain, and he wouldn't have taken the time if he had it. HEART members weren't in it for recognition or glory. They weren't in it for money. Most were in it for redemption, for a chance to make sure no one else ever lived through the pain they'd experienced. Cyrus was no exception to that.

"I take it you're not going to fill me in?" She brushed thick strands of hair from her cheek. He hadn't turned on a light, but the darkness couldn't hide the paleness of her skin, the narrow width of her shoulders. She looked more vulnerable than he wanted her to, more delicate than Essex's description had led him to believe.

"Later. Right now, we have more important things to do." He pulled an energy bar from his pocket, handed it to her. "Eat."

"I don't think so." She thrust it back. "I've already been drugged a couple of times. I'm not going to let it happen again."

"It would be stupid for me to drug you right before we make a run for it."

"Run? You know how far it is to the nearest town?" she asked.

"Seventy miles."

"Exactly. Running is *not* going to be an option."

"Leaving is. That's the plan. How we do it is going to depend on whether or not I can turn off the security system before John shows up." He walked to the window that looked out into the church's front yard. Moonlight spilled onto the lush grass. A few shrubs lined the path that led from the church to the residential area of the compound. Someone stood beside one of them, his shadowy form nearly blending with the dark outline of the bushes.

John. Cyrus didn't have any doubt about that.

"Is he out there?" Lark asked, leaning in so that she could see out the window. He doubted she realized how close they were or how vulnerable she was making herself. If he'd wanted to take her out, he could have done it easily.

"Yes."

"Where?" she whispered as if John might somehow hear.

"Near the shrubbery. Right at the edge of the path."

"What's he doing out there?"

"Making sure I do what he's paying me to do. It's not going to be long before he comes in to check on my progress. Come on." He took her hand, pulled her away from the window.

"Where? There isn't a place on the compound without security cameras. If we leave the building, he'll know it."

"I can take out the security cameras."

"How?"

"How about you save the questions for later?" He strode through the sanctuary and into a narrow hall. The church office was to the left, the door closed and locked. It took seconds to get in, just a little longer to log on to the computer. He typed in the password that John was a little too careless with, smiled as the security system opened up to him.

Lark stood a few feet away, watching intently as he began typing in code. "You're a man of many talents, Cyrus."

"Not many, but the ones I have are useful in situations like this."

"Would they be useful in opening this?" She pointed to a file cabinet.

"If it was necessary."

"It's necessary," Lark responded, tugging at the handle.

He ignored her. They didn't have time to play seek-and-find.

"Cyrus," Lark said, waving a hand in front of his face. "Did you hear me? I said it was necessary."

"Your idea of necessary and mine aren't the same. To me, necessary is shutting down the security system and getting us both out of here in one piece."

"You've been on the compound for how long?"

"About a week."

"So, you've seen the trucks coming and going in the middle of the night?"

"Yes."

"And you're not curious? You don't want to know what's in them?"

He sighed, looked up from the computer screen and met her eyes. Gray eyes. That's what Essex had said. It was hard to tell from the photographs and impossible to see in the darkness.

"Yeah. I'm curious, but not so curious that I'm willing to die to find out."

"It will only take a—"

The sound of a door opening silenced her and made every nerve in Cyrus's body jump to life.

Footsteps tapped on the tile floor, John's toneless whistle filling the church.

Cyrus flicked off the computer, turned on a light, nearly tossed Lark into the chair.

"Play along," he hissed.

She barely had time to nod before John was there, moving into the room, his dark gaze jumping from Cyrus to Lark and back again.

"What are you doing in here?" he snapped.

"Getting the information you asked me for," he said coldly.

"The door was locked for a reason, son."

"I'm not your son, and you said to bring her wherever I wanted, do whatever was necessary."

"I didn't mean break into the church office."

"Then, you should have been clearer. Fact is, this is the farthest away from people that we can get. You don't want anyone hearing her, right?"

John hesitated, something in his face going just a little soft as he looked at Lark.

"Right," John finally said.

"Then how about you go, and leave me to do what I do best?" Cyrus offered his best predatory smile, the one that had made tougher men than John back down.

"I think I'll stay. If you're such an expert at getting information, I might learn something from you." He dragged a chair over, sat it right in front of Lark.

"You're going to tell us what we want to know. Right, doll?" John said. "You're going to make this easy on everyone. It's what Joshua would have wanted."

"I guess you'd know," she replied. "You were one of his best friends." There were freckles on her cheeks and nose, dark circles under her eyes. She was closing in on thirty, but could have passed for twenty, her dark red hair curling around an unlined face.

Delicate.

That's how she looked.

Maybe that's why John leaned forward, touched her cotton-skirt-covered knee. "You took something that belongs to Elijah. Where is it? All you have to do is tell us, and you can go back to your life."

"Like Joshua was allowed to go back to his?"

"Joshua died in a terrible accident," John said with a scowl. "The police investigated. They agreed."

"What about Ethan?"

That was a name Cyrus hadn't heard before, and he forced himself to relax, to let the conversation play out. There was a lot going on that he didn't understand, and that could be dangerous.

John's scowl deepened. "He's probably living life somewhere far away from Amos Way."

"He would never have left his wife and children."

"He was always looser in his morals then the rest of the group. Joshua knew that. You knew that."

"What I know," she said quietly, "is that you're a pawn in whatever game Elijah is playing, and that you're paid plenty of money to be one. You betrayed the group. You betrayed my husband. You're the reason why he's dead. I don't know if you pulled the trigger or if one of your hired men did, but—"

"Shut up!" He lunged toward her, his fist raised, his intent obvious.

Cyrus had no choice.

He pounced, tackling John to the ground, struggling as the other man reached for his gun, tried to free it from its holster. John was strong and outweighed Cyrus by a good seventy pounds, but if he won, it was all over. No backup was coming. No help was on its way. For the first time since Cyrus had joined

HEART, he was on his own. It was the way he'd wanted it. He had a feeling he was going to regret that choice.

He wrestled John into a choke hold, managed to keep him from freeing his gun. Was panting hard, trying to force him into submission when something heavy whizzed by his head, glanced off his shoulder, slammed into John's face.

There was a grunt, a crash. And then there was darkness.

THREE

Lark stumbled across the dark room, slammed into a chair that blocked the path to the door.

She pushed the chair out of the way, raced to the door. Escape. That's all she wanted.

But Cyrus had risked his life for her, and running meant leaving him behind. Injured? She didn't think so. She'd tossed the lamp at John's head, saw it make contact a split second before the room went dark. At least, that's what she thought she'd seen. She wasn't sure. Her hands had been shaking. Her body had been shaking, all the adrenaline and fear pouring out. She might have missed her mark, seen what she wanted to see rather than what was.

She reached the door, could have run through the hall and out back, raced through the cemetery and climbed the fence, been in the woods and heading toward civilization in minutes.

But she couldn't leave Cyrus.

No matter how much her brain was screaming that she should.

She ran her hand along the wall, found the light switch and flicked it on. Turned to face the men.

Cyrus knelt beside John's prone body, his eyes dark, his expression unreadable. He looked tough and hard, his black security jacket hanging open to reveal his shoulder holster.

"Is he dead?" she managed to ask, her throat so tight she barely got the words out.

"Not even close." He took the handcuffs from his belt, turned John onto his stomach, yanked his arms up behind his back and cuffed him.

"I hope I didn't hurt him too badly."

"I hate to tell you this, Lark, but hurting McDermott is the least of your worries." He removed John's gun belt. "You know how to use a firearm?"

"Yes." Joshua had taught her to load a rifle and a handgun, and she'd become a decent marksman in the years she'd lived in Amos Way. Owning firearms, understanding how to use them, that was part of a sustainable lifestyle, part of self-reliance and living off the grid. It had been a while since she'd been out shooting, but she hadn't forgotten.

"Put this on." He thrust the gun belt into her hands.

Obviously, he wasn't worried about her using the gun on him.

She took the belt, buckled it around her waist. John wasn't a small guy, and she wasn't a big woman. Especially not now. Three months in Amos Way reliving all the good times and that one really bad time, a week in the prison trailer avoiding drugged food, and she'd lost any extra weight she'd ever had on her.

The belt slid to her hips, and she pulled it back up.

"Come here." Cyrus grabbed the front of the belt, dragged her close, used his knife to dig a hole through thick leather. "Try that."

It was perfect.

Of course.

Cyrus seemed like that kind of guy. The guy who never made a mistake, who didn't hesitate, who knew exactly what needed to be done and how to do it.

He opened a desk drawer, rifled through it. Opened another one.

"What are you looking for?"

"Keys. Elijah's car is parked just outside the gate. We might be able to use it."

"Only if we can get out of the gate without

being shot," she responded. Elijah was the only member of the group allowed to have a car. The other vehicles were kept in a large garage built two decades ago. Her in-laws kept an old Cadillac there. Her car was there, too, the old Ford Mustang parked close to the garage doors, the key handed over to her father-in-law when she entered the compound. No way did she plan to go back to her in-laws' place to look for it. She wasn't going back for her notebook either. Maybe she should. She'd written notes in it, kept track of every delivery to the compound and every shipment that left it. That had to be the key to understanding Joshua's death, and until she understood it, she couldn't move forward, couldn't move on.

"No keys anyway," Cyrus said, closing the last drawer. "No phone. There's no external internet connection on the computer. It's networked with the ones in the security barracks, but there's no access to the outside world."

"Are you sure?"

"I snuck in here a few nights ago to check."

"There's a phone in Elijah's house."

"We're not going to risk going there."

John moaned, turned onto his back, his eyes open but unfocused.

"We could take him with us," she suggested. "He could probably get us a ride out of here."

"Get us killed you mean. We've got two guns and two people. The security team is ten times as strong. And I can tell you from bunking with them for a few nights, they couldn't care less about their fearless leader." He logged on to the computer, typed a password in. "If Elijah gives orders to take us down, they're not going to care if John goes down with us."

She hadn't thought about that, but he was right. Elijah led the pack. John followed his orders. "We could break into one of the storage units. All the hunting rifles and ammunition are kept there." Along with whatever had recently been delivered. She wouldn't mind getting a peek at that while they were there.

"Too risky."

"Without risk there can be no great reward."

"You sound like Essex," he muttered, his fingers flying over the keys. She didn't know what he was doing, but a code seemed to be forming on the computer screen.

"Thank you."

"Did I say that was a compliment?"

"Doesn't matter if you did or not. I like Essex. He's a great guy." She took the knife from the sheath that hung from John's gun belt, used it to pry open the file cabinet.

There wasn't much in it. Just alphabetized birth and wedding certificates.

She closed the drawer, glanced around the room.

"You're not going to find what you want here," Cyrus said.

"What do you know about what I want?"

"You want to shut Clayton down."

"True."

"You want to prove he had your husband killed. Or that he pulled the trigger."

"Also true."

"You should have gone to the police. Asked for professional help."

"I did. They needed evidence that a crime was committed. Something more than just my gut instincts."

"You came back to find it?"

"I came back because my in-laws asked me to visit." Looking for evidence had been a side product of that.

"Right." He continued to type rapidly, his attention seeming to be completely focused on what he was doing.

"It's true. They sent a couple of letters at the end of the school year, asked if I had any photographs of Joshua that they could have."

"I thought this place frowned on cameras and photographs and all those modern type things."

"It does, but Elijah made an exception because my mother-in-law, Maria, was grieving so much. I made some copies of our wedding photos and brought them with me."

"You're more naive than Essex thinks if you believe your in-laws wanted you back here for photographs."

"I had my own reasons for coming back." And she *had* believed her in-laws. At first. Later, when there'd been excuse after excuse for keeping her at the compound, when she hadn't been allowed access to computers, cars, the outside world, she'd realized she was a prisoner. She hadn't tried to escape. She'd been too focused on her goal to worry, too sure she'd be able to find the evidence she needed to be very concerned.

That was its own kind of naïveté.

Or maybe stupidity.

Fortunately, it hadn't gotten her killed.

Yet.

"You do realize that we're trapped in a compound with a dozen armed men who aren't going to want to let us escape, right?" she asked, stepping to the door and looking out into the hall. The church was still silent, the hallway and the sanctuary beyond it dark. That didn't mean they were safe. In Amos Way, nothing was ever what it was supposed to be. Even her in-laws weren't what they'd claimed. They'd told her she was a daughter to them, that they loved her as much as they'd loved their own children. She doubted they'd have let one of their kids rot in a trailer for five days.

"I am very aware of our situation," he responded calmly.

"Then, maybe you could hurry?"

"If I hurry and type in the wrong thing, we're sunk."

"We're sunk anyway," she muttered.

"Essex didn't tell me you were a pessimist."

"I'm a realist." And realistically, she couldn't see any way out of the mess she'd gotten herself into.

Faith. That's what Joshua would have said. Faith and God could move mountains.

She'd tried to hold on to that after he'd died. Mostly she had. There were days when she struggled, when she wondered why God's plan included pain and heartache. On days like that, she had to remind herself of the good times and the blessings.

"Got it!" Cyrus pushed away from the desk, grabbed her hand and dragged her out into the hall.

He moved so fast, they were out the back door and in the old cemetery before she could think about the danger. Moonlight shone on crumbling headstones, casting long shadows across overgrown grass and weeds. The fence was a few hundred yards ahead. She'd climbed it before, in the first heady months of marriage when she and Joshua had been giddy with happiness, when they'd thought they'd live in Amos Way for a few years, teach school there, repay Joshua's college debt to the compound and then move on with their lives.

They'd had it all planned out. Once upon a time.

She tripped over gnarled weeds, nearly landed face-first in the fence. She grabbed the chain link, started scrambling up it without any prodding from Cyrus. They were on limited time. Eventually someone would realize the cameras were down, sound the alarm and the compound would spring to life, all Elijah's security force rushing to find the reason why.

She reached the top of the fence, realized she didn't have a jacket or coat to throw over the barbed wire.

"Here." Cyrus tossed his coat over the jagged barbs.

She scrambled over the top, the barbs poking

through the coat, the alarm finally sounding, screaming its warning through the still night.

Cyrus should have found a way to take out the alarm, but he hadn't wanted to take the time to do it. Lark had been right about the number of armed men and their chances of surviving. They needed to move quickly, stay a step ahead of the men who would be tracking them. On his own, he could have done it easily. He wasn't so sure about managing it with Lark. She was moving well, up and over the fence without a problem, but adrenaline would wear off eventually. When it did, she'd be done.

He needed to get them away from the threat before then.

That wasn't going to be easy. No car. No phone. No means of communication with civilization. The closest highway was a few miles away, the rural road that led to it too obvious a means of escape. There'd be security guards there in minutes, blocking any chance of using that route.

He clambered over the fence, grabbed his coat as he climbed down the other side.

Lark was just ahead of him, moving at a fast jog, heading straight for the road.

"Wrong way." He snagged the back of her

sweater, headed in the opposite direction, towing her along with him.

"We need to get to the road," she protested. "We might be able to get a ride from someone."

"How many cars use that road, Lark?"

"Not many."

"None. Unless they're heading here," he corrected. He needed her completely committed to his plan, absolutely determined to do things his way.

"You never know," she replied. "Sometimes people get lost. Sometimes they turn onto the road and make it all the way to the compound before they realize they're heading the wrong way."

"And sometimes it snows in April, but not often enough to count on. The woods are a better choice."

"The road is the quicker, straighter route out."

She was persistent, he'd give her that, but he was calling the shots from now until they made it to safety. "If we want to die. I don't."

She was silent after that, stumbling along beside him as he ran toward edge of the woods that spread out from the border of the compound. He'd studied maps before he'd arrived. He knew how deep the woods were, how secluded Amos Way was. Built on land that had once housed a logging business, the compound was surrounded by thousands of acres of deep forest. To the north, fifty miles of wilderness fed into federal land. To the east, more woods and an abandoned ski lodge. From there, they could access the highway. They just had to make it across twenty miles of forest.

The siren shut off abruptly, and Lark grabbed his arm, her fingers cold through his shirt. She was shaking, and he dropped his coat around her shoulders, knowing it wasn't the cold that was getting to her.

"It's okay," he tried to reassure her, but she had to know it wasn't okay. They were in trouble, and if he'd had a cell phone, he'd have called the team, brought in the cavalry.

He didn't have a cell phone, didn't have any hope of backup.

He had nothing but himself, enough years and experience to get them through, and the kind of tired worn-out faith that probably should have been buried years ago.

He'd held on to it, though. It was the one thing he had left from the time he'd had with his parents. They'd believed with everything they were that God had a plan, that He'd lead them in the right direction. That direction had led them to the Congo and mission work that had gotten them killed and his sister kidnapped.

Cyrus had been twelve, left with the pastor of their church because his parents had thought he was too young to travel to the Congo.

When they'd died, he'd been angry, but he didn't blame God. They'd put themselves in a dangerous situation for the sake of people they didn't know.

He couldn't fault *them* for it either.

He knew what it was like to willingly go in where others wouldn't, to risk everything for a stranger. Like his parents, he'd committed his life to saving others. Only he wasn't saving souls. He was saving lives. And, he wasn't pulling a family into it, wasn't going to leave anyone behind if he was killed.

A dog howled. A second joined it.

Lark's grip tightened and she glanced over her shoulder, her hair flying out in a mass of tangled curls. He should have made her tie it back, because it was bound to get caught on branches and limbs as they moved through the dense forest. There wasn't time now.

"Looking back isn't going to change anything," he said quietly.

"It's going to keep me from being surprised when the dogs lunge."

"They're still in the compound."

"They won't be for long."

"Which is the best reason for moving forward instead of looking back."

"Stop being reasonable and smart, Cyrus. It's annoying when I'm working up to full-out panic." She slid her arms through his coat sleeves, her hands trembling as she tried to zip it. He brushed her fingers away, had the zipper up in seconds.

"If you panic, we're both sunk, so you're going to have to hold things together until we get somewhere safe."

"I don't know how safe River Fork is. The town has ties with Amos Way."

"Do they?" That was something he hadn't known, and it wasn't something he was happy to hear.

"Elijah grew up there. His half brother is the town sheriff."

"You think he's dirty?" He shoved through thick foliage, holding back a heavy pine bough as Lark stepped past.

"I don't know. He ran the investigation into my husband's death."

"And ruled it accidental?"

"Yes."

"You think he was covering up for someone?"

She hesitated. "I don't know. He presented

his findings to me and my in-laws. It all sounded good."

"But?"

"Maybe I just don't want to think my husband could have been careless enough to clean a loaded rifle."

"Or maybe Elijah's brother helped him get away with murder?"

She didn't respond.

He wasn't sure if she was thinking about her answer or if she was too tired to speak. Her breath panted out, hoarse and raspy and a little too ragged for his liking. They had a long way to go. All of it on foot. If she couldn't make it, he'd have no choice but to stay and fight. He didn't have enough firepower to have any hope of success against Elijah's security team.

He'd try, though.

If he had to.

He prayed he wouldn't, the words forming and taking flight before he'd even realized the depth of his desperation. He wanted out of the woods and away from Amos Way, he wanted a safe place to hunker down and come up with a plan. He might not know what was going on in Elijah Clayton's religious utopia, but he planned to find out. When he did, he'd take the man and his followers down without a second thought or a moment of regret.

There were too many wounded people in the world searching for places to belong. Amos Way wasn't the kind of place they should end up, because it was the kind of place people never returned from. In his estimation, that was the kind of place that should be shut down for good, and he was just the kind of guy to do it.

Behind them, a dog howled, the sound too close for comfort.

A man shouted something, and Cyrus grabbed Lark's hand, dragging her into a full-out run.

FOUR

She wasn't going to make it. Not if they had to run the seventy miles to town. Lark was as sure of that as she was that Elijah's men were closing in on them. She could hear voices in the distance, dogs barking. They had a head start, but it wasn't enough of one.

"We need to split up," she managed to gasp, the words rasping out into the chilly night air.

"That would be a stupid decision, and I don't make those," Cyrus responded. No emotion in his voice. No sign that he was stressed, worried or frantic. He didn't even seem winded. Whatever HEART was, whatever his job before he'd come to Amos Way, the guy was cool as a cucumber and in top physical shape.

"It wouldn't be stupid for you. Without me holding you back, you can probably outmaneuver Elijah's men."

"I'm not here for me. I'm here for you, and I'm not leaving you behind." He veered to the left, seemed to be leading them back toward the compound, and Lark had a moment of doubt, a moment when she wondered if his help was all just some bizarre game that Elijah wanted to play.

She stopped, her body trembling with fatigue and adrenaline. All she wanted was to find a way out of the woods and back home. She wanted to walk into her little apartment, sit on the love seat she'd bought when she'd moved back to Baltimore, forget that she'd come to Amos Way for a reason and that she hadn't fulfilled it.

She couldn't do it, though.

Not even after they got out of the woods.

If they got out.

Cyrus was suddenly in front of her, his hand on her upper arm. "We need to keep moving."

"Not if it means going back where we came from. I may be in bad shape, but I know we're heading toward the compound."

"You hear the dogs behind us?" he asked as if there were some way she couldn't. The hounds were howling, their frantic barks warning that they'd caught the scent of their prey.

"Yes. And, I don't want to walk into them. Which is what we're going to do if we turn around."

"Trust me, Lark, I don't want to run into

them either. We're going to do a wide arc around the compound and come out in front of it. If we're careful, we should be able to get into the garage and hot-wire one of the cars."

It sounded good. If it was true, it was a reasonable plan. Probably the best chance they had of escaping. She didn't like it, though. She'd finally gotten out of the compound. She didn't want to be anywhere near it again. Didn't want to risk being caught and dragged back. If she was, there'd be no second chances at escape.

"Lark," Cyrus growled, the edge in his voice coinciding with the sounds of pursuit that seemed to fill the woods. "We don't have time for this. You want to freak out and do your own thing, wait until we've got a few dozen miles between ourselves and this place." He grabbed her hand, and she let him pull her into an all-out run. Somehow, he managed to avoid crashing through foliage, snapping branches and making the noise she seemed to be making. She wanted to tell him to slow down so she could move more quietly, but her lungs burned, her throat so dry from heaving breaths that she couldn't get the words out.

He slowed abruptly, going from a dead run to a walk, leading her through a small thicket that she'd been in one night a lifetime ago. She looked up as they passed through, saw the same starry night sky that she'd seen when she and Joshua had lain on a wool blanket and talked about their future and their dreams. She shivered, her teeth chattering and her body shaking.

"It's okay," Cyrus whispered so quietly, she almost didn't hear him.

The words weren't comforting.

She would have told him that if they hadn't been closing in on the compound. She could see it up ahead. Someone had turned on the generator that powered searchlights. A beacon for the lost, Elijah had explained when she'd questioned the positioning of the lights, the fact that they illuminated the woods that surrounded the compound rather than the compound itself.

She hadn't believed it.

There'd been a lot she hadn't believed. A lot she'd wanted to believe.

She'd believed in Joshua, though. She'd believed that what they'd had would last a lifetime. She'd believed they'd have decades together, that they'd share thousands of wonderful memories.

Cyrus's grip on her hand tightened, and he tugged her close, wrapped an arm around her shoulder.

"Hold it together, Lark." He breathed into her

ear, the words ruffling her hair and pulling her from the memories.

She jerked away, put some space between them.

She had no idea who Cyrus really was.

She only knew what he'd told her. Words were easy and they were cheap. They were lies nearly as often as they were truths. She'd learned that the hard way, and she wasn't going to forget it. She was sticking with Cyrus because the only other option was going it alone, and she had about as much chance of surviving that as she did of taking a vacation on the moon.

He didn't pull her back, didn't tell her to stay close as they slipped through the forest just out of reach of the spotlights. They should be hurrying. The dogs would be tracking their scent back toward the compound soon. When they did, their handlers would report back, let John and Elijah know that their prey was returning.

Cyrus had to know that, but he moved like they had all the time in the world.

"We need to hurry," she whispered, the words pushed past the hot lump in her throat.

"We need to be quiet," he responded.

"The dogs—"

"Shhhhhh!" he warned as they stepped out of the trees and onto a dirt road shrouded in shadows. No spotlights here, but she knew exactly where they were. Up ahead, the garage stood in the middle of a cleared field. No trees. No bushes to hide their approach. It seemed like an eternity since she'd driven her car across the clearing, parked it in the far left bay, handed her keys to her father-in-law. She'd planned to stay two weeks. Tops. She was closing in on three months. Was the car still there? Or had Elijah gotten rid of it? He sure hadn't planned to let her return home. She knew that. Did her father-in-law? Her mother-in-law?

"See that tree?" Cyrus motioned to a huge pine tree that jutted up from the edge of the forest. "I want you to wait there."

"For what?"

"I'm going to get in the garage and hot-wire a car. It's going to take a few minutes."

"Minutes?"

"I've done this a couple of times," he responded, giving her a gentle push toward the tree. "Hurry up. We're running out of time."

"I'm coming with you." No way was she going to stand near a pine tree, hoping for the best. If Cyrus got in the garage and managed to start a car, she planned to be right there with him.

"It's too dangerous," he insisted, his eyes flashing in the darkness.

"For me but not for you?"

"For both of us, but it's my job to take the risk."

"We're wasting time arguing about it." She headed across the clearing, heard him mutter something under his breath as he followed.

Cyrus wanted to drag Lark back to the tree line, but she was right. They were wasting time. The garage was just ahead, dark and silent. No sign that anyone was nearby. He snagged the back of Lark's sweater. "Let me take the lead."

She nodded, moving to his left, letting him walk a few steps ahead. In the distance, the dogs barked frantically. How long before one of Elijah's men realized that he and Lark had headed back toward the compound? The young guys were mostly paramilitary thugs who had delusions of grandeur. Trained in underground militia groups, they had no idea how to track deer let alone human beings. They were dogged, though, and he doubted they had much in the way of moral codes. Loyalty to the highest bidder. That seemed to be the theme of Elijah's security force. That made the men unpredictable and not easy to control. That was one of the reasons Cyrus had been invited into the group. His military training gave him a leg up, his experience making him perfect leadership material in John's eyes. Getting inside the compound had been easy. Getting out was going to be complicated. He'd gotten out of worse situations, but he'd always had a team to back him up.

He reached the six-bay garage. The lock was rudimentary. Elijah obviously wasn't all that worried about having vehicles stolen. Why would he be? They were out in the middle of nowhere, the citizens of Amos Way were followers who seemed to like the strict rules they lived by.

Lark touched his arm, her fingers light and tentative. "I parked my car in the far left bay. It's an old Ford Mustang. I didn't lock the doors. Should be pretty easy to hot-wire, if you know how."

He did. He also knew how to pick locks, hack into computer systems and pretend to be a hundred people he wasn't.

It took seconds to open the garage bay. The building was filled with cars, each bay four or five cars deep. He didn't use his flashlight. No sense calling attention to themselves. But he could see the hulking bodies of a few old trucks and several ancient Cadillacs.

Lark's Mustang was a 1967 muscle car. Not practical for the kind of dirt road driving that was required to reach the compound. The doors were unlocked, and she climbed in the passenger seat, silent, pensive. He could feel her anxiety as he went to work, could feel his own anxiety building. Every beat of his heart was a reminder that time was ticking away, that Elijah's men would circle back around eventually. Probably sooner than Cyrus would like, sooner than he needed them to.

He took a utility knife from his belt, opened the ignition switch on the car. His hands were steady, his mind focused, but he could hear the dogs in the background. They were getting closer.

He stripped the wires, held them together.

The engine started, and he stepped on the gas, revved it.

It coughed and sputtered. Stalled out.

"Come on," he muttered, touching the wires again, repeating the process.

The engine sputtered, died. Again.

"We need to get out of here," Lark said, an edge of panic in her voice.

She was right, but going on foot wasn't going to work.

Elijah's men were too well armed and too determined to stop them. He didn't let himself lose focus, couldn't allow himself to think of anything but that moment. Touching the wires together again, revving the engine. It caught the fourth time, kept running as he put the car into gear.

"Thank you, God," Lark whispered.

Cyrus almost told her that they weren't home free yet, that they had a long way to go before they were safe.

No sense raining on her parade.

Or scaring her more than she already was.

He let the car roll out of the garage, knowing that the sound of tires and engine would carry on the quiet night air. Out here, there were no cars driving by, no traffic creating white noise. There was nothing but the sound of nature. When that was interrupted, everyone in the community noticed it.

As soon as he cleared the garage, he stepped on the gas. The car responded immediately, jumping forward with so much speed the tires spun. It was a nice ride. One Cyrus would have appreciated more if he weren't expecting trouble.

He knew they were only minutes ahead of their pursuers. If Cyrus was fast enough, he'd have just enough time to get to the end of the dirt road before the security team caught up. Once they hit the paved road, it was a three-mile drive to the interstate. There'd be traffic there. Not much this time of night, but enough to put some cars between the Mustang and

Elijah's team. Unless they wanted a fight with the local police and the state PD, they'd back off and let Cyrus leave.

Trees brushed the sides of the car, but he didn't have time to be careful. His headlights splashed across the rutted winding road, reflecting off trees and a guard rail that separated the road and a small creek that ran to the west of the compound. He'd been there a couple of days ago, fishing with a few of the men who provided food for Amos Way. They hadn't been part of the security team. They were members of the community who had given up everything to live secluded from worldly influences. Good, God-fearing men who didn't seem to have a clue that their compound was being used as a front for something else. Strange, because it had taken Cyrus all of three days to realize that Essex's missing friend wasn't the only thing being hidden in Amos Way.

Of course, he was more cynical than most people, more suspicious than most. It came with his past, with his military career, with his job.

He'd still felt guilty for playing the men for fools, because that's what they'd think he'd done. They'd been accepting, kind, showed him the ropes of fishing and asked him about his life. He'd lied about his past, given the background HEART had created for him. He'd listened while one of the men had shared the gospel, obviously concerned for Cyrus's eternal salvation. Then, he'd turned the conversation around and picked their brains, tried to get a feel for what was going on under the surface of the compound.

A conversational thief. That's what his colleague Stella liked to call him. A master at moving a conversation in the direction he wanted it to go without anyone realizing he was doing it. It was a good tool to have in his line of work, and he wasn't going to give up doing it. He just wished he hadn't been using it on a couple of guys who'd have probably been his friends in other circumstances.

In *these* circumstances, they'd probably stand by and watch while Elijah's security team shot him.

Community over self.

He had to keep that in mind. The people of Amos Way seemed innocent and oblivious, but they were indoctrinated to believe that Elijah's word was nearly the same as God's.

Not cool. Not in any situation. In this one, it could prove to be deadly. If he and Lark were caught, there'd be no second chance at escape.

Behind them, lights splashed on the dirt.

Nothing more than a curve in the road separated them from the security team. It was tempting to pull over, get out, stage an ambush. He could take out the tires of the vehicles, but he couldn't take out the gunmen. Not all of them. Not before he or Lark was hurt.

Or worse.

He accelerated, taking a curve too quickly, the tires spinning in dirt and dead leaves before finding traction again. He could hear Lark's breathing, hear her frantic gasps. She didn't scream, though. Didn't ask questions. Didn't do anything but sit stiff and tense in her seat, eyes trained on the road in front of them.

He glanced in the rearview mirror, saw a black sedan rounding the curve he'd just taken. It was a straight stretch to the paved road. Nothing between him and the car behind.

Not just one car. Another sped around the curve. Probably four or five armed men in each.

They were going all out to keep Lark from escaping.

Because of what?

What did she have or know?

There were a dozen questions he wanted answers to, but he wouldn't get any of them until they were out of danger.

The headlights splashed on blacktop, and his heart jumped.

Almost there. Just a few hundred yards, and then three miles.

He sped out onto the paved road, taking the turn so quickly, he nearly lost control.

Slow it down. That's what his colleague Jackson would have been saying. *Stay focused.*

Cyrus would have been ignoring him and everyone else on the team. Not that he didn't respect the other members. He did. He was used to making split-second decisions, trusting his instincts to get him through. Right now, his instincts were saying that the cars behind them weren't the only things he needed to be concerned about.

If Lark was right, the sheriff of the closest town had connections with Amos Way. It was possible the danger behind them was chasing them into even more danger. If Cyrus was arrested on some trumped-up charge, Lark would be alone. That would be a perfect opportunity for Elijah to take her down.

He wasn't going to let that happen.

He had to get to a phone, call in the team, get some backup.

First, he had to lose their tail.

He pressed the accelerator to the floor and sped along the road, heading toward the interstate and their only hope of escape.

FIVE

Lark clutched the door handle, her gaze on the side mirror. She could see the headlights of the oncoming car. The Mustang was fast, but she didn't know if it was fast enough to outrun a modern car. She'd never tested it out, never been tempted to drive above the speed limit, find out the Mustang's mettle. She'd bought it when she was in high school, and she'd spent a good amount of money making sure it stayed running. After she'd married Joshua, the car had been stored in the Amos Way garage. She'd retrieved it after his death, driven it to Baltimore, slept in it for a few too many nights, because she'd barely had enough money in her account to buy food and gas let alone rent a place.

She loved the old car, but she loved her life a little more. If pushing it to its limits burned the engine out, so be it. As long as they got to the highway before that happened.

"Can you go any faster?" she asked, her heart thumping painfully. Her body seemed to be vibrating with the force of it, and she had to clench her teeth together to keep them from chattering.

She'd been scared plenty of times in her life, but this was the stuff of nightmares. A pitch-black road, headlights behind them, nothing but darkness ahead. Certain death if they were caught, but not much of hope of escaping.

Her eyes were dry from staring so long without blinking, but she was afraid if she did blink the car would be on them, bullets would be flying. Cyrus might lose control of the Mustang, drive it into the ditch on the side of the road.

"Breathe," Cyrus said so quietly she almost didn't hear.

"What?" she tried to ask, but she had no breath in her lungs, no air to push the words out.

"Slow breaths, Lark. In and out, because if you pass out and fall into me, we're both going to be in trouble."

Breathe. Right.

The body was supposed to do that automatically. Hers seemed to have forgotten how. She took a gasping breath and then another, realized that she was clutching the door handle so tightly, her nails were cutting into the leather.

"I'm okay," she said as much for herself as for Cyrus.

"I know you are."

"And I was breathing." Just not regularly.

"Okay," he said, his eyes focused on the road, his attention fixed exactly where she wanted it to be.

"They're still behind us," she pointed out just in case he'd missed the bright lights on the road behind them.

"Another thing I didn't need to be told," he responded drily.

"Do you need to be told that there's a stop sign about a hundred yards straight ahead?" she asked, her gaze fixed on the sign and the intersection beyond it. No merge onto the interstate. This was supposed to be a full-out stop.

He didn't respond, didn't seem to let up on the gas.

One minute they were approaching the intersection, the next minute they were in it, tires spinning as he took the turn too quickly, righted the Mustang and just kept on going.

"Are you crazy?" she nearly shouted. "You could have gotten us killed. You could have killed someone else!"

"There was no one coming."

"There could have been!"

"Do you think I would have risked your life

and the life of another driver? I don't do things unless I'm as sure of the outcome as anyone ever could be."

"How would I know what you would or wouldn't do? I don't know you, remember?" She glanced in the mirror. No lights. Not one car was on the road behind them. "They're gone," she said, almost afraid to say it out loud for fear that the lights would appear again.

"I noticed." If he was happy about it, she couldn't tell. His expression was hard, his jaw set. If she'd seen him in an alley somewhere, she'd have run the other direction. But there she was, letting him drive her Mustang while she sat in the passenger seat and hoped he was one of the good guys.

"You're not surprised?"

"No."

"Can you elaborate?"

He nodded, his hands relaxed on the steering wheel, his gaze still focused on the road. "You said that Elijah's brother is the sheriff of River Fork."

"Half brother."

"River Fork is the closest town. Elijah knows that. He's probably already called his brother to let him know we're on the way."

"So we'll go to Smithville. It's a dot on the

map, but it's only twenty miles farther. There's a gas station, a phone, a—"

"We're almost out of gas. I'm sure Elijah knows that, too."

"I had half a tank when I gave my father-in-law the keys." She leaned across the seat, looked at the fuel gauge. From her angle, it looked like they were already on empty. "Someone syphoned the gas or drove the car around without permission."

Cyrus shrugged. "The reason is irrelevant, because it doesn't change anything. We're going to need gas. Thanks to Elijah's rules about not having money at Amos Way, neither of us can pay for it."

"Don't you get paid to be part of the security team?" She'd been told the security team got paid well. Why else would so many young men stay in a place with such strict rules?

"The money is deposited into my bank account, but I don't have access to it unless I'm out of the compound. My wallet, cell phone and electronics were collected when I entered Amos Way. Just like yours were."

"So, you're driving without a license?"

He laughed, the sound rough and a little harsh. "I think that's the least of our worries."

He was right, but it was a lot easier to worry about that then about the nearly empty fuel tank, their moneyless state, Elijah's half brother waiting for them to show up in River Fork.

If he *was* waiting.

She'd spoken to Sheriff Radley Johnson several times in the weeks following Joshua's death. He'd been kind, empathetic, seemingly determined to uncover the truth. In the end, he'd said that there hadn't been evidence of homicide and no obvious motive for someone in the compound to want to harm Joshua.

She'd tried to convince him that Joshua was too careful to have made such a rookie mistake, but he'd been unable to reopen the case without evidence to prove that the death was more than an accident. Unable or unwilling? That's what she'd wondered when she'd decided to return to Amos Way.

She was wondering it even more now that they were heading straight for the sheriff's jurisdiction.

If Elijah had called ahead, asked his brother to stop them, that would explain why the security team had given up the chase.

She squeezed the bridge of her nose, trying to stop the pulsing pain that was building behind her eyes. It had been months since she'd had a full-out debilitating migraine. Usually, the first hint of one and she took the medicine she'd been prescribed.

But Elijah didn't believe in medicine. He didn't allow pain relievers, instead he encouraged his followers to pray for healing, expected that they would avoid doctors. There were a few rare occasions when a member of the community was granted permission to seek medical treatment, a few times when an accident required a trip the emergency room.

Elijah hadn't made any exceptions for Lark. He'd confiscated her medicine before she entered the compound, refused to allow her to see a doctor when she'd had a fever a couple of weeks ago.

Not surprising, since she didn't think he'd intended her to ever leave Amos Way.

Pain shot through her eye, and she tried to will it away. She had to focus, but her thoughts were like mist on a lake. There. Gone. No way to hold on to them. No way to form a coherent plan that would get her out of the mess she'd gotten herself into.

She wiped a sweaty palm on her skirt. The road stretched out into the distance, shimmering black in the headlights. No one in front. No one behind. This was a quiet stretch of road, and she knew it well enough to know there weren't houses lining it. No enclaves of civilization dotted the area. Just trees and mountain views.

"So, what are you thinking?" she asked, because the pain in her head made her want to close her eyes, let him handle everything. But that wasn't who she was. It wasn't how she dealt with life. "That we're going to drive until we run out of gas and then hitchhike to town? Beg a phone from someone there?"

"We're both carrying firearms, and you're wearing—" he gestured to her skirt "—that. People are going to notice us if we hitchhike. If the wrong person notices, the sheriff is going to be called."

"What's the plan?"

"There's a gas station a half mile outside of River Fork. We'll go there. See if we can talk the attendant into lending us a phone. I'll probably have you do that." He shot a look in her direction, the gaze quick but assessing. "You're less intimidating than I am."

She wasn't intimidating at all, and she knew it. She was shorter than some of the fifth graders she taught, smaller boned than most women she knew. She'd never let that stop her from standing up for herself or demanding what she was due. She didn't have the energy to tell him that. Plus the pain in her head was shooting sparks of light in front of her left eye. She swallowed bile, tried to concentrate on the conversation. "You want me to call Essex? Ask him to come get us?"

"No way. He has a wife and a couple of kids. I don't want to drag him into this mess. I'll give you my boss's number. Chance can have a team here by dawn."

"A team from HEART." She repeated the name he'd given her, tried to pull information about it from her pounding head.

"HEART is a business, but we're like family. I put in a call, and I'll have help. Simple as that. We just have to get to the gas station and get access to a phone before we run out of gas or Elijah's men catch up to us."

"You think they're still following?" She shifted, looked out the back window.

"No, but I thought finding you and making sure you were okay was going to be easy. I was wrong about that. Another error in judgment could get us both killed. Like I've already said, I'm not planning to die."

There was nothing to say to that.

Even if there had been, she wasn't going to expend the effort to say it. She felt sick, the migraine taking hold, wringing every thought from her head. Not a good situation to be in, but she'd been in worse. She touched the raw spot on her wrist where she'd cut herself with the nail. She'd made it through the darkest hours of her captivity. She'd make it through this.

Once she did, once they were safe, she'd turn her attention back to the original goal. She'd known all along that Elijah wasn't the kind of person to be messed with. He had power and money. She wanted to know where the second came from. Not just from the odd jobs and sale of goods produced by the Amos Way community. Not from the bank accounts of the men and women who'd signed their life savings over to the community. The money came from somewhere else, and there was a lot of it. Once she found out the source, she could pull the plug and close down Amos Way for good.

She felt a twinge of regret at the thought. Her in-laws loved the place. They'd spent half their lives there, but that didn't mean it was a good place or even a decent one. As much as she hated to take their home from them, she'd do it if it meant stopping Elijah.

She wouldn't let him murder anyone else. She wouldn't let him get away with the crimes he'd already committed.

She owed Joshua that. She hadn't been able to save him, hadn't been able to convince him to leave Amos Way before it was too late, but she could do this for him. She would do it.

Or she'd die trying.

And the way she felt right then, death was a distinct possibility.

Lark's silence worried him, and Cyrus didn't need more worries to add to the list he already had.

They were in the weeds, and he needed to find a way to get out of them. He had a plan A, but nothing else. If his plan didn't work, they were sunk.

He scowled, glancing in the rearview mirror. A semi was moving up behind them. No sign of Elijah's men, though. Nothing that would make him think they'd been followed.

Which worried him, too.

If he'd had his cell phone, he'd have already called Chance Miller, told him he needed help. Hopefully whoever was manning the gas station would be amiable to the idea of lending a phone. If not, Cyrus would have to find another way to contact the team.

Lark leaned her head against the side window, her movements jerky and disjointed. She hadn't closed her eyes, but she looked like she needed to, her face a pale oval, her eyes glassy.

"We've got another half hour ahead of us," he said. "Why don't you try to get some sleep?"

She didn't respond.

"Lark?" He touched her arm, and she shifted away, rubbing the spot where his hand had been.

"I'm okay."

"You don't look it."

"I am. At least, I'm okay enough to do whatever we have to do," she mumbled, the words sluggish and slow as if every one of them took effort.

"What we have to do is survive, and that's not going to happen if you don't trust me enough to tell me what's going on."

"What is going on," she responded, enunciating every word, "is that my head is going to explode from a migraine. I don't have medicine with me, so there's nothing I can do but ride it out."

Not good for her or for them.

"What can I do to help?" he asked.

"Stop talking?" she suggested.

"Okay."

"You spoke again," she groaned, throwing her arm over her eyes. "And every word is like a thousand knives being shoved into my eye."

He didn't know much about migraines, but he knew plenty about headaches. The improvised explosive device that had nearly taken his life had led to months of debilitating headaches. He wasn't plagued with them anymore, but he'd never forget how they felt.

She groaned again, shifting so that her head was buried in her elbow, her hair falling across her arm.

He smoothed strands of it from her neck, slid his fingers to the pulse point beneath her jaw, felt the slow steady beat of her heart beneath cool clammy skin.

"I'm not dying," she muttered. "I just feel like I am."

The comment surprised him almost as much as the wry smile she shot in his direction. Even sick as a dog, she had a sense of humor and an easy smile. That was one of the things Essex had mentioned. That Lark was likable, the kind of person who filled up a room with her smile, who made others comfortable, would drop anything to help a friend.

Cyrus had been surprised by his army buddy's high praise of a woman who wasn't his wife, and he'd asked point-blank what Lark was to Essex. He'd been put in his place, told flat-out that Lark was the little sister Essex had never had and that if Cyrus thought anything else, he could forget the debt that he owed Essex and move on with his life.

That wasn't going to happen. Cyrus always repaid his debts.

Besides, he'd believed Essex. The guy was a family man through and through. He loved his wife with a loyalty and passion Cyrus admired. He was also smart and savvy about people. Which was why Cyrus had agreed to go to Amos Way. He'd still been more than a little convinced that Lark was just another lonely soul who'd decided to join a cult to gain connection and acceptance. People did it all the time. Cyrus contacted a few every year—men or women or teens who'd decided to separate themselves from loved ones so that they could follow a charismatic leader who called them family.

Now that he'd met Lark, he knew the truth. She wasn't the kind of person who'd follow anyone blindly.

She shifted, throwing her arm over her eyes and leaning her head back against the seat. He wanted to tell her that one of the members of HEART was a nurse, that when he called, he'd ask her to bring medicine to help with the migraine, but he didn't think she'd appreciate the words any more than a promise of help that wasn't going to come for hours.

The semi passed, whirling by at high speed. Cyrus wanted to drive just as fast, but he couldn't risk being pulled over for speeding. He had no license, and he didn't want to be locked up in the county jail while he waited for the authorities to run a background check.

Slow and steady. That was the way to do things. Keep focused on the mission, on the goal. Don't veer from the plan unless absolutely necessary.

He chugged along the highway, going exactly the speed limit, the Mustang a smooth ride despite its age.

The drive seemed to take forever, but he reached the gas station in just under an hour, pulling into the well-lit parking lot and driving around to the back of the building. That lot wasn't visible from the road, and that mattered since they might be waiting for a while.

"Finally." Lark sighed, straightening in her seat, her hair tumbling around her shoulders. She had a lot of it, and he wanted to brush it off her cheeks and out of her eyes.

"I thought you were sleeping."

"It's kind of hard to sleep when a knife is being stabbed through your eye over and over again." She opened the glove compartment. "What's the plan?"

"We go in and ask for a phone."

"Together?" She dug through some papers, pulled out a rubber band and pulled her hair into a ponytail. "Don't you think we'll get more attention that way?"

"Probably, but I'm not going to leave you out here, and I'm not going to let you go in alone. That doesn't leave a whole lot of options."

"Too bad pay phones are obsolete. I probably have enough change under these seats to make the phone call." She leaned forward, winced. "Never mind. If you need change. You can look."

He got out of the car, rounded it and opened her door, lights from the building illuminating Lark's paper-white face.

"You're not looking so hot," he said, taking her hand and helping her out of the car.

"Just what every woman wants to hear from a good-looking guy."

"Compliments, Lark?" he asked. "You're obviously in worse shape than I thought."

"Not a compliment. A statement of fact. I am a woman. You're a good-looking guy. Of course, being a woman doesn't mean I need or want to be told I look good. Being good-looking doesn't mean you're anything more than a pretty face."

"Pretty, huh?" He reached for the gun belt she still had strapped around her waist, unhooked it and unloaded the pistol. "I know it's cold, but I'm going to need my jacket back until we're done in here. I walk in with my gun belt showing, and we'll lose any chance we have of borrowing a phone."

"Pretty," she responded as she unzipped the jacket and handed it back to him.

He slipped it on, dropping the ammunition into his jacket pocket and setting her gun and belt on the floor of the backseat. "Don't say that to my team. They'll never let me live it down."

"I'm sure they already know it."

"Maybe, but they wouldn't dare say it to my face," he responded, closing the door and taking Lark's elbow. "If we're asked any questions, we're out of gas and money, and I'm calling a friend for some help. Maybe we'll get to use the phone and get offered a couple of gallons of gas to get us on our way."

He led Lark around the side of the building, stopped under a streetlight. The light highlighted a dark bruise on Lark's cheek, the blood that stained her wrists. There was a rip in her skirt, dirt smudged across her sweater, leaves caught in her hair. She looked exactly like what she was—an escapee. She also looked a decade younger than he knew she was, vulnerable and in danger.

"We need to do something about this," he said, tugging her sleeves over her wrists, pulling a small twig from her hair. "The cashier is going to get one look at you and call the police."

"I can wait out here."

"Not in a million years." He glanced through the front window of the small gas station convenience store. The attendant was behind a counter, staring at his cell phone. Young. Maybe late teens or early twenties, he seemed intent on whatever he was doing. "The restroom is to the left of the door. Walk in behind me and head straight there. Hopefully the guy behind the counter won't care enough to ask questions. If he does—"

"I'll tell him I ran from Amos Way. That you picked me up on the road, and that you're trying to help me get home. I'll ask to use the phone, and tell him that I want to call a friend to come get me."

She was quick on her feet. Even with a migraine.

He opened the door, stepped into the store, Lark pressing close to his back as she moved in behind him. The kid at the counter glanced their way but went right back to his cell phone. Lark hightailed it down a little hall that led to the bathroom.

So far, things were working out just the way he'd planned.

He approached the counter, waited until the young man looked up again.

"Help you?" the kid asked.

"I hope so. My cell phone battery is dead, I'm out of cash and I'm almost out of gas."

"Not allowed to give freebees to anyone." The kid ran a hand over his hair, his attention on his phone again.

"I wasn't planning to ask for one. I know times are tough. I was just wondering if I could borrow a phone to call a friend."

The kid frowned. "I don't know…"

"It will take me two minutes, and then I'll be out of your hair."

"My boss doesn't like anyone in the office, and that's where the only landline is."

"I'm stranded man, and I've got my girl with me. You know how bad I'm starting to look? No gas? No phone? No money?"

The kid hesitated, his gaze shifting to a point beyond Cyrus's shoulder, his eyes widening.

"That your girl?" he asked, and Cyrus turned.

Lark walked toward them, her hair down, her face and hands clean. She'd pulled the sleeves of her sweater over the cut on her wrist and had used the rubber band to cinch her sweater in the back. She must have rolled the waistband of her skirt. Instead of ankle-length, it hit her right at the knee. She still looked done-in, her eyes shadowed, the bruise on her cheek obvious, but she didn't look like an escapee from Amos Way.

"Yeah," he finally responded, slipping his arm around Lark's waist.

"You hit her?" the kid asked. He might be young and more interested in his phone than his job, but his concern was obvious. "Because that wouldn't be cool, man. I'd have to do something about it."

"I don't hit women," he responded at the same time Lark laughed.

"He wouldn't dare. I tripped and fell into a door." She touched the bruise, shook her head ruefully. "I might need to take some lessons on walking."

The guy smiled, obviously charmed by Lark. "You and me both. I broke my foot last year walking off a curb. You can go ahead and use the office phone. Office is down the hall past the restroom. Door is unlocked."

"Thank you," Lark said smiling, and Cyrus thought it would be pretty easy to be charmed by someone like her.

He touched her back, was urging her to the hallway when headlights splashed across the storefront window. Cyrus's pulse jumped, and he looked outside, saw a police cruiser idling there.

Could have been a coincidence, but Cyrus wasn't willing to wait around to find out.

"The police," Lark whispered as if he could have missed the car.

"Let's make sure we're not seen," he responded, hurrying her into the office and closing the door behind them.

SIX

No windows.

That was the first thing Lark noticed.

The second thing she noticed was the phone sitting on a small desk against the far wall.

Cyrus had the receiver in hand before she took a step toward it. He dialed, his gaze focused on the door.

Was he expecting the police to barrel in?

Lark sure was.

Her head throbbed with every movement, the sharp pain behind her eye making her dizzy and sick. She couldn't afford to give in to either. She pressed her ear to the door, tried to hear past the pulse of blood in her ears. Nothing. She was tempted to open the door, look out into the hall. As if seeing the threat coming would make things better.

The only thing that would make things better was going back in time, making a different decision, staying in her Baltimore apartment rather than returning to Amos Way.

She had a little too much confidence in her own abilities.

That's what Essex had said before she'd left town. He hadn't wanted her to go, had said he'd had a bad feeling about the trip. He'd even tried to get his wife Janet to talk her out of going.

She hadn't listened.

Stubborn as a mule, that's what Joshua would have said. He'd have said it with a smile, and she'd have smiled in return. She knew because they'd had the same conversation dozens of times during their marriage.

Old memories. Good memories.

Almost all her memories of Joshua were.

"You still with me?" Cyrus asked, his hand settling on her shoulder.

"I'd rather be somewhere else, but yeah. I'm here."

"That's the spirit," he responded, reaching past her and turning the doorknob.

"What are you doing?" she gasped, terrified the police would be standing on the other side.

"Standing here isn't getting us anywhere. I'm going to see if the police came inside."

"And, what am I supposed to do?" she asked, grabbing his arm when he would have stepped into the hall. "Wait here for whatever the duration of your jail sentence is?"

"I'm not planning to go to jail."

"I wasn't planning to be held captive at Amos Way, but I was," she responded, not releasing her grip on his arm. "If a police officer is out there—"

"Lark, we can stand here and discuss this all night, but it's not going to change the situation. My boss has already sent some people our way. They'll be here in a few hours. If I get arrested, you ask the kid at the counter to give you a ride into town. Wait at a diner or in the library, somewhere where you won't be alone. Someone from HEART will find you there."

"But—"

"I don't think I'm going to be arrested. That's a 'just in case.'" He gently removed her fingers from his arm and strode down the hall like he didn't have a concern in the world.

Lark had plenty of them.

If he was arrested, there was no way she was going to wait around town for some strangers to show up and save her hide.

She grabbed the phone, tried to think of someone who would drop everything to come to her rescue.

Essex would have, but Cyrus was right. She couldn't pull him into her trouble. Other than him, there was no one. She had friends, but most of them were married with kids. Most had busy schedules, hectic lives. They were friends but only in the most perfunctory way. Lark's fault. She'd kept herself busy since Joshua's death. Too busy for things like coffee with friends, nights out on the town. She didn't enjoy the party scene, had no interest in double dates. She'd been happy with her job, with her coworkers, with church and the charity work she did.

None of those things were benefiting her now, so maybe she should have spent a little more time building relationships and a little less time trying to forget the past.

She set the phone down, walked out into the hall, heard the murmur of voices. Not raised. Just quiet conversation. She didn't know who was talking, and she didn't dare creep to the end of the corridor to look. An exit door stood at the far end of the hall, and she ran to it, her stomach heaving as pain shot through her head. She wanted to sit on the floor, close her eyes, let whatever was going to happen happen. She'd never been a quitter, though, had never known how to give up without a fight.

She opened the door, stepped out into darkness. Cold air bathed her cheeks, and she inhaled deeply, trying to fill her lungs and clear her head. The night smelled of wood-burning fire and rain, the moisture in the air seeping through her sweater. Straight ahead, a small copse of trees separated the gas station from the lights of distant houses. River Fork. It was a half-mile walk. An easy one. If she wasn't being hunted.

She wrapped her arms around her waist, moved away from the building. If she made it to town, she could ask someone for help. There were plenty of elderly women in River Fork, and she doubted any of them would turn her away.

She couldn't leave Cyrus, though. Not without being certain that he was okay.

She pressed close to the building, and eased around the corner. She could see the front parking lot from her vantage point. A police car was parked near the front door, lights off, doors closed. Not the sheriff's patrol car. This one was a state trooper's vehicle.

She wasn't sure if she should be relieved or terrified.

Elijah had connections in law enforcement. She knew that. She just wasn't sure how deep those connections went, how far they reached.

The shop door opened, and a police officer stepped outside, a bottle of soda in hand. He took a sip as he walked to his vehicle. If he was looking for someone, he wasn't acting like it. He leaned against the hood of the car, gaze focused on the highway. A few cars sped by as he took another swallow of soda and yawned.

She could only see the back of his head and torso, the police emblem stitched to the shoulder of his jacket, the gun holster that peeked out from beneath black leather.

Was he waiting for someone?

Elijah maybe? One of his men?

She wanted to ease farther into the shadows, hide herself in the darkness, but she was afraid to move. There were pebbles and debris littering the ground. If she kicked something, moved it with her foot, accidently knocked into the building, the officer would turn and see her.

A lifetime seemed to pass while he drank the soda, every beat of her heart throbbing behind her eye. She'd never passed out from having a migraine, but she felt like she might. She couldn't sit, didn't dare sit. Too much noise, and she didn't want to have to explain who she was or why she was sitting on crumbling pavement in the shadow of the gas station store.

Finally, the officer got in his car and drove away.

She needed to go back inside and find Cyrus. He wouldn't be happy that she'd slipped out the door. She didn't care. She'd done what she'd thought she'd had to, taken care of herself and her safety the way she had hundreds of times before. She reached the side entrance, tried to open the door. Locked.

"Perfect," she muttered. "You took care of yourself and got into trouble like you have hundreds of times before." She tried the door one more time because she didn't want walk around to the front of the building, walk in the front door, have the kid behind the counter question how she'd gotten outside without being seen and why she'd felt the need to do it. The door hadn't miraculously unlocked itself in the two seconds since she'd tried it the first time. Which left her with no choice but to go in the front door.

"Great," she whispered, turning back the way she'd come. To her left, the copse of trees was dark as pitch, the leaves rustling in a rain-filled breeze. Something moved at the edge of the blackness, a darker darkness against the tree line.

She froze, eyes probing the shadows, brain trying to register what she was seeing.

Tree?

Bear?

Man?

It moved again. Quickly. In a sudden rush

that had her sprinting toward the corner of the building.

Too late.

It was on her. He was on her. Hand on her mouth, arm around her waist, hot breath ruffling the hair near her ear. "You shouldn't have run, Lark."

The voice filled her with cold terror.

John.

She tried to pry his fingers from her mouth, tried to wrest herself out of his grip. He was strong, and she was exhausted, all the days and nights in the shed without food making her weak, the migraine making her weak.

"Stop fighting me," he growled. "I don't want to hurt you. I told you that before. I just want what Joshua took from Elijah."

He took nothing.

He gave me nothing.

I know nothing.

She couldn't get the words out past his tight grip, so she just kept tearing at his fingers, elbowing his gut. All the things she'd learned on the streets of Chicago.

She slammed her head into his chin, felt his grip loosen, slammed it back again and was shoved with so much force she hit the side of the building and fell backward. She landed with a thud that sent pain shooting through her eye, scrambled to her knees, expecting John to be in front of her, dragging her back up again.

He was gone. Back into the trees? There wasn't a hint of movement in the darkness.

She stumbled to her feet, her body stiff and sore, her muscles tense. Did he have his gun trained on her? Was he planning to—

Someone grabbed her arm, and she screamed, turning toward her attacker, fists flying as she screamed again and again.

Cyrus managed to grab one of Lark's fists before it hit his throat. He snagged the other as she went for his nose.

She was in full-out panic, her eyes wide, her face devoid of color. He doubted she was seeing anything but her own fear, didn't think she was hearing anything but the pulse of blood in her ears.

"It's okay," he said, keeping his voice calm, his tone gentle. He'd been mad as a hornet when he'd realized she'd left the store, but confronting her now wasn't going to help either of them.

She tugged frantically, trying to free herself.

He wasn't going to let her go, but he didn't want to hurt her either. He pulled her arms down, holding her hands close to her sides. They were inches apart, her chest heaving with the fear and exertion, her eyes wild in the darkness.

He leaned down so they were face-to-face, nearly nose to nose. "I said it's okay," he repeated.

She blinked, stopped struggling.

"Cyrus," she said, and he nodded, running his hands from her wrists to her shoulders, afraid she might fall over if he didn't support her weight.

"Were you expecting someone else?" he asked.

She took a deep shuddering breath.

He felt it through his palms, felt her gathering strength and courage and all the things that had gotten her through the time she'd spent in Amos Way.

"John was here," she finally said, her voice trembling. He felt that, too—all her terror, her fear. It made him angrier than he'd been when he'd seen the empty office, realized she'd left. It made him want to pull her in close, promise that things were going to be okay.

He didn't do that kind of thing.

He wasn't the guy to reassure and offer comfort. Jackson Miller was good at that. Boone Anderson was good at it. All Cyrus knew how to do was act.

Right then, he wanted to hunt John down, drag him to jail and have someone lock him away.

"Where?" he asked, probing the shadows,

searching the darkness, his body vibrating with the need to move.

"He was over near the trees." She gestured to a small grove that separated the gas station from an old country road that led to town. He could see distant house lights and streetlights, the small quaint town pretty and inviting. Even at night. Even when everything else looked bleak and lonely.

"You're sure?"

"I've known him for years, Cyrus. There was no mistaking who he was."

"Did he hurt you?" he asked.

"No. He asked me to give back what Joshua took."

"What did he take?"

"I have no idea."

"You're sure?" He needed her to be certain, because whatever it was had to be the key to what was going on in Amos Way.

"I'm sure." She was shaking harder, her teeth chattering.

He unzipped his jacket, dropped it around her shoulders, his fingers brushing her nape.

"Thanks," she murmured, and he nodded.

"Aside from asking for whatever he thinks you have, did John say anything?"

"He said he didn't want to hurt me."

A lie. They both knew it, so there was no

sense pointing it out. "Didn't want to hurt you, so you shouldn't force him to by withholding information?"

"That was the gist of it. He disappeared right before you arrived."

"He must have heard me coming." And run off like the coward he was. Without a dozen men backing him, John wouldn't confront Cyrus. That was the type of guy he was. More than willing to bully people weaker than him, but not willing to take a stand against someone who could bring him down.

"It's odd," she said, pulling the edges of his coat closed and burrowing her chin into the collar. "He was alone. As far as I could tell, the team wasn't with him."

"I don't think he wants to call attention to what he's doing," he responded, scanning the tree line. If John was there, he'd hidden well. Cyrus could have tracked him, but that would have meant leaving Lark.

"I guess if I were trying to kill people, I wouldn't want to call attention to it either," she responded, her voice still shaking, her body trembling so violently, his coat slipped from her shoulders.

He pulled it back into place, held it there as he looked into her eyes. "Trying to kill *me*. Not you. He wants to take me out. He wants something from you. He won't be able to get it if you're dead."

"Is that supposed to make me feel better?" she asked.

"If you're interested in staying alive, it should."

"I'm interested in *both* of us staying alive."

"That's a nice sentiment, Lark, but sentiment doesn't keep people from dying."

"So, you're saying that if John returns with an army of security members, it's every man for himself? You'll fight for your life and I'll fight for mine?" she asked, hands on her hips.

"If he comes back, I'll fight for you. You'll fight for you. Between the two of us, we should be able to keep you safe."

"Who's going to keep *you* safe?" she asked.

"I'm pretty good at doing that myself," he said, taking her arm and leading her around the side of the building. The Mustang was running on empty, but there might be enough fuel to get them to Main Street. If not, they'd walk, hugging the shadows and staying out of sight. It would take a half hour tops. They'd have another four to burn before Stella and Boone arrived. Chance had researched the area, found a small diner that was open all night. It wasn't an ideal place to wait things out, but it was better than being a half mile outside town sitting in the empty lot of a gas station.

"I'm pretty good at doing it, too, Cyrus," Lark said as she lowered herself into the passenger seat, reached into the back and retrieved the gun. "But even people who are good at taking care of themselves, people who have always kept themselves safe, need help sometimes. I learned that while I was lying in that trailer praying that God would send someone to help. It wasn't a fun lesson, but I'm not going to forget it anytime soon. I'm not going to forget that you were the one He sent either. And if you're ever in trouble, if you're ever at the point where you really do need someone to step in, I can guarantee you that I'll be the first to show up."

She closed the door before he could respond.

It was for the best. Cyrus wasn't sure what he would have said. The cold hard facts were that Essex had sent him to find Lark. No mystery there, no supernatural intervention. Nothing but a guy who cared contacting a buddy who could help. But there was more to life than fact. More to any situation than the simple easy explanation. He'd learned that working at HEART. Jackson and Chance Miller were hardcore former military men. They knew how to fight. They knew how to win. Somehow, they also knew how to trust in something beyond themselves.

That had been difficult for Cyrus to accept, and even more difficult for him to understand. Up until he'd begun working for Chance, he hadn't believed in much more than a faraway God who barely checked in on His people.

In the past few years, he'd discovered something different. Faith was the secret ingredient that turned hopeless situations into salvageable ones, that made people who thought there was no way out look for a way.

He didn't have to ask to know what had kept Lark going during the dark hours of the night when there was no one to hear her cries, no one to help her.

He slid into the driver's seat, started the engine, pulled out of the parking lot and onto the road that led to town. No security cameras there. No houses. Nothing between them and town but the narrow road and the trees that lined it. If they were going to be ambushed, this was where it would happen.

Nothing moved, but his skin crawled, the hair on the back of his neck standing on end. Someone was watching. If it was John, he had a gun, and he wouldn't hesitate to use it. Not if he thought it could get him what he wanted.

The first shot exploded through the back

window, whizzed by Cyrus's head and lodged in the windshield.

"Get down!" he shouted as he stomped on the accelerator.

Lark dropped down, but she didn't stay down. She reached into his coat pocket, pulled out the clip that he'd taken from the handgun.

"What are you doing?" he demanded.

"Making sure he doesn't follow us," she responded as she unrolled the window, leaned out and fired a round into the street.

SEVEN

It had been two years since she'd fired a handgun.

Two years since she and Joshua had stood in the practice field at the east edge of the compound, loading, firing, loading again. He'd drilled her on safety, insisted that she know everything there was to know about firearms.

She'd been eager to learn because she'd loved him.

She'd never expected the knowledge to come in handy.

She squeezed the trigger again, aiming for the road behind them. No cars there. No chance that she'd hit someone. She didn't want to hurt John. She wanted to scare him into backing off.

"We're almost at the town limits," Cyrus said, the words gritty and rough.

He wasn't happy.

She didn't care.

She'd told him the truth. She wasn't going to

be content to stay safe while he put himself in danger. She'd do her part. She'd take as many risks as he did, as many as were necessary to make sure both of them made it out alive.

"Unload and put the gun away," he continued.

"He might—"

"You want to be a team, then you follow orders, Lark. The orders are to stand down. We've got houses coming up. You want to kill some kid who's sleeping in bed?"

"I'm not a fool," she said, settling back into the seat and removing the clip. She shoved it into her pocket, put the gun in the glove compartment. John wasn't a fool either. There was no way he'd attempt a shoot-out in town. If he was following them, he'd keep his distance, bide his time until he could take Cyrus out and bring Lark back to Amos Way.

An image flashed through her mind, the picture so vivid, she gagged. Blood on the floor. Blood on the wall. Joshua lying facedown, his fingers limp on the butt of his rifle.

She closed her eyes, but the image was there, embedded in her brain.

Cyrus touched her hand, his fingers warm and dry against her cool, clammy skin.

"Breathe," he said like he had before, and

her airways opened, oxygen flooding lungs she didn't know were starved for air.

"Again," he commanded, and she inhaled, exhaled the memories.

"I'm fine," she managed to say even though her insides were shaking, her head pounding.

"You're also good with a handgun," he responded, his hand slipping away from hers. She felt cold in its absence, her bones aching with it. She pulled his coat around her, but it didn't ease her chill.

"My husband taught me."

"From what I've heard, he was a good guy."

"Who did you hear that from?" she asked, but she wasn't surprised that he'd heard about Joshua. People in Amos Way had loved Lark's husband. He'd been raised in their midst, had come back to teach their children. He'd supported the community, espoused its ideals and agreed with the foundational beliefs it had been built on. They hadn't known about his doubts, they'd had no idea that he'd planned to fulfill his obligation, pay the community back for his college education and then leave. He'd loved the people in the compound, but leaving to achieve his education had changed him. In the end, it had gotten him killed.

"John. He needed a reason for locking you up. He told the community that you'd gone a little crazy after Joshua's death, started breaking into houses, stealing things. He said he couldn't blame you for it. Joshua was one in a million."

"He *was* one in a million," she responded, her eyes burning, her throat tight.

"We all are, Lark," he said quietly. "There isn't one of us who doesn't have something unique to offer the world. I'm not taking anything away from your husband, but it seemed odd to me that John sang his praises so loudly. He isn't the kind of guy to praise anyone."

"They grew up together. Were as close as brothers."

"Do you think John pulled the trigger and killed your husband?" he asked, the question blunt and unapologetic. Unlike other people who learned that she was a widow, he didn't seem to mind probing Lark's wounds.

She nodded, the pain in her head exploding into a hundred tiny knife points stabbing through her skull. "Yes."

"Did you tell the police that?"

"I told them that I didn't think he'd shot himself. There was no evidence to prove that I was right. It looked like an accident. They assumed it was."

"But you think differently."

"Joshua…changed the last six months we were at Amos Way. He was quiet and withdrawn. Up until that point, we'd shared everything. No secrets between us. It was one of the rules of our marriage." She smiled a little thinking about it, remembering how young and naive they'd been. So in love and so convinced that their love would be enough to get them through anything.

"Did you ask him about it?" he asked as he passed the River Fork welcome sign.

They'd made it to town. She should feel relieved, but she just felt tired, sad and sick. "So many times that we both got tired of the conversation."

"And?"

"He said that he didn't want me to know. He didn't want anything to happen to me. I wanted to leave the compound, but he insisted that he had things under control."

"What things?"

"One of his really good friends had been questioning some of Elijah's policies. Ethan didn't like the way the compound's finances were being handled."

"You mentioned Ethan before." He stopped at a quiet intersection, turned left onto Main Street. The town slept peacefully, streetlights illuminating pretty yards and 1940s bungalows. She and Josh had only visited River Fork a handful of times. Elijah didn't like community members to be too exposed to the excess the world had to offer. Simple lives spent relying on God and on each other. That's what he offered the people who found Amos Way. It had all sounded so nice when Joshua had described the little community.

"Ethan," she said, "is the key to everything. He called a council meeting and demanded that Elijah give an accounting of how community funds were being spent. Elijah agreed, but Ethan disappeared before it happened. He went missing during a hunting trip. A few of the guys had heard him talking about leaving Amos Way. Most people assumed that's what happened. He went on the hunting trip and just walked away."

"Very convenient for Elijah."

"That's what Joshua said. He seemed to be the only one saying it. Everyone else was content to believe that a family man, a guy devoted to his wife and kids, would leave them."

"And no one else was interested in forcing Elijah to account for the community funds, right? Your husband started digging around, he made people uncomfortable and then he died in an accidental shooting?"

"Right," she responded, her voice raspy and hot. She hated talking about what had happened to Joshua, hated the memories that were always just a thought away.

"I'm sorry, Lark," he said as he pulled into the parking lot of a small diner.

Everyone was sorry when they heard the story, but sorry couldn't change it. Sorry couldn't bring Joshua back. It couldn't bring Ethan back.

"When are your friends arriving?" She changed the subject because that was easier than continuing down the path they were going.

"Their ETA is four-thirty. If Stella is driving, they'll be here sooner. If Boone is, they'll be here on time." He turned off his headlights, drove around to the back of the building and edged the Mustang in close to hedges that butted up against the lot.

"So, we're just going to sit in the car and wait?"

"I'm going to sit and wait." He eased the jacket from her shoulders, used it as a blanket, draping it over her torso. "You're going to rest. Put the seat back. Close your eyes."

That wasn't going to happen.

Not while she was still conscious and breathing.

"Do you really think I could lie here and sleep knowing that John is stalking us?"

"I think you could try."

"The way I see things, two sets of eyes are better than one. If John tries to sneak up on us—"

"I'm a good bodyguard and an ace shot. If John shows up, I'll take care of him."

"If he shows up, I don't plan on sleeping through it," she replied, her skin crawling at the thought of John creeping across the parking lot, sneaking up behind them, aiming his gun.

"Suit yourself," Cyrus responded, his eyes black in the darkness, his lashes long and thick. She'd said he had a pretty face, but it wasn't pretty. Not by a long shot. He looked tough and confident, determined and just a little dangerous. Not the kind of guy she'd ever liked to spend time with. She'd always preferred men who were more subtle in their masculinity. Strong but not overpowering, able to take care of themselves and the people they loved but without the rough edges and tough veneer.

"You're staring," she pointed out, shifting uncomfortably.

"So are you."

"I'm trying to figure out what you want." Everyone wanted something. It was a lesson she'd learned from watching her mother jump from one bad relationship to another, one self-absorbed loser to another.

"I want to repay my debt to Essex."

"And?"

"Does there have to be more?" He brushed strands of hair from her cheek, his fingers glancing across the tender spot near her jaw. "If there does, then I'll just say that I want to get you home in one piece and I want to make sure you stay that way. That means bringing Elijah Clayton down. So, I guess I want that, too."

"What do you want for you?" She wanted to swipe her hand across her cheek, wipe away the warmth that lingered where his fingers had been.

"Who says I want anything for me?"

"Are you going to tell me that you don't?"

"How about this, Lark? You tell me your secrets, and I'll tell you mine."

"What's that supposed to mean?"

"That we all have something we're hiding. You fell for Joshua when you met him in college. You were both intelligent, both hardworking, you could have settled anywhere, done anything, but you decided to get married in Amos Way, live there, teach there."

"Joshua had an obligation to pay the community back for his college education. He'd promised to return and teach at the schoolhouse."

"Promises are as easily broken as they are made."

"Not by Joshua."

"Maybe not, but he could have found another way to pay the debt. He would have. If you'd wanted him to."

"You never even met him. You have no idea what he'd have done," she bit out, the migraine pulsing furiously behind her eye, her stomach constricting. She hated that he was right, but he was. She'd thought the same thing a thousand times since Joshua's death, lived with the guilt of the choices she'd made.

"I know what it's like to be in love," he countered. "I also know what it's like to live with regrets. Yours aren't going to change anything."

He'd hit the nail on the head, pinpointed exactly why she'd returned to Amos Way even though she'd known she shouldn't, even though that still small voice had been whispering that she should stay away.

Her stomach turned, and she knew she was going to be sick. Right there in the Mustang she and Joshua had used during college, the one they'd driven to Amos Way, music blasting from the stereo, voices mingling with the songs that were playing.

She opened the door, fell out onto the pavement, dry heaves tearing from her gut as her palms skidded across the blacktop. She didn't feel it, didn't feel anything but the horrible pounding pain in her head and gut-twisting ache of her empty stomach.

He was an idiot.

It was as simple as that.

Too focused on the goal to realize he was pushing too hard.

Cyrus crouched beside Lark, pulled her hair back from her face as she retched. She had nothing in her stomach, but her body heaved, her muscles jerking with the force of it.

He held her shoulders, kept her from slamming her head into the pavement. There was nothing much else he could do but hold her steady and keep his eyes on the shadows. They were vulnerable there, hidden from the street but easy enough to see if someone was looking.

A cold breeze sent leaves skittering across the pavement, a dog barked, a car engine revved. Life went on around them, but at the dark edge of the parking lot, it was just the two of them.

She took a deep shuddering breath, jumped to her feet, probably would have fallen down again if he hadn't slid his arm around her waist, pulled her into his chest.

"Slow down," he ordered, sliding his hand up her spine, urging her to lean into him. She stood in his arms, stiff and unyielding, every muscle in her body tense.

"Relax. I don't bite," he ground out, his hand kneading the tense muscles at her nape.

"I just want to go home," she responded so softly he almost didn't hear.

They did something to his heart, those words. Made him think of things he was better off forgetting. Made him remember that hot humid night in Colombia. Megan Wallace lying on the ground. He'd touched her jugular, felt the thready pulse, known she didn't have long, known that the mother who'd sent HEART to find her would never see her alive again.

Your mother loves you, he'd said, even though he hadn't thought Megan could hear. *She wants you to know it.*

I love her, too, she'd said, her eyes opening for one brief moment. *But it's time for me to go home.*

He shook the memory away, refused to allow it to play through his head.

Most missions were successful. Some were not.

It was best to stay as unemotional as possible, keep his mind focused and his feelings in check.

Lark deserved something more than emotionlessness, though. She needed something more.

She'd lost her husband. She'd lost faith in a community that was supposed to be a religious nirvana. She'd been given a rough shake, and now she was with him—a guy who knew nothing about softness, nothing about gentleness.

"I'm going to get you home," he said, breaking every rule he'd made for himself after Megan's death. He'd promised her mother that he'd bring her home, he'd vowed that Amber Wallace would have her only daughter back. He'd been high on himself, too arrogant to realize that he had limited control, too foolish to understand that the days of a person's life were numbered before she was born, and that there wasn't one thing he could do to add or subtract from anyone's allotted time.

No more promises.

That's what he'd decided after he'd called Amber with the news about Megan's death. No deep emotional involvement. That was what he'd vowed as he'd stood at Megan's grave, watched her coffin lowered into the ground and listened to her family sob.

"*We're* going to get me home," Lark responded, her voice faint, her body still stiff in his arms.

"To start, let's get you back in the car." He kept his hand on her waist, steered her to the Mustang.

She didn't say a word as she lowered herself into the seat, wiped her palms on her skirt. Blood smeared across the fabric, and he lifted her hand, turned her palm so he could see the damage. Bits of gravel and dirt had gauged deep scratches in her palm.

"I'm a mess," she said, pulling her hand away, wiping it on her skirt again. "But there's nothing I can do about it until your friends get—"

The sound of a car engine interrupted her words.

Not Boone and Stella. It was way too soon for them to arrive.

Lights flashed across Lark's pale face, and her eyes widened. "It's the sheriff," she whispered, all the horror, all the fear of seeing that car reflected in her eyes and in her voice.

"Let's see what he has to say," he responded, turning to face the police cruiser as it pulled up beside them.

EIGHT

The sheriff looked nothing like Elijah's half brother.

That was Cyrus's first thought as the guy got out of his cruiser.

His second was that he looked tough. No softness in his face. No excess weight on his belly. He looked fit and ready for a fight.

"Cyrus Mitchell, right?" the sheriff said without preamble.

"Depends on who's asking," he responded as he got out of the Mustang.

"Sheriff Radley Johnson. I got a call from a friend of yours. Said he wanted to make sure you stayed out of trouble."

"What friend?"

"Chance Miller. He says you work for him."

"That's right." He didn't offer anything else. It would be just like Chance to check in with local PD. It's what he did when the team was going into areas where they might accidently step on toes. This situation was different, but if Chance had done some digging and found the sheriff to be on the up-and-up, he might have called and asked Johnson to step in.

Until Cyrus heard from Chance, he wasn't going to trust the guy. Even after he heard from Chance, he probably wouldn't trust Johnson.

"You've had some trouble out at Elijah's place." A statement of fact rather than a question, the sheriff's gaze moving from Cyrus to Lark and back again.

"Also right," Cyrus admitted. There was no sense lying about it. The sheriff hadn't just happened upon them. Either Chance really had called him and told him where they were, or John had sent him out hunting for them. Either way, the guy knew what was going on.

"We'll go to the station and discuss things there." Again. Not a question. Not a suggestion either.

"If I refuse?"

"I could arrest you," Johnson responded. "But that'd be a lot of paperwork I'm not in the mood for doing. So, how about I just make your options really clear. You and your friend come with me, we sit down in my office, have some coffee and some of the cookies Agnes Renee brought in and figure out what's going on. Or, I can leave you two sitting here waiting for whoever shot out the back window of this car to show up. Eventually, I'll end up back here, and you'll either end up in jail until we prove self-defense or you'll end up in a body bag."

Cyrus wasn't keen on either option, but he'd spent a lot of years trusting his instincts. Right now, they were saying that heading to the station with the sheriff was a better option than sitting in a parking lot waiting for John to show. Besides, he was getting that skin-crawling feeling again, the hair on his arms standing on end.

"I can tell you exactly who shot out that window," he offered, and the sheriff nodded.

"I figured you could. You can file a report when we get to my office."

"You want me to follow you over?"

"I heard you were out of gas, so how about we all go together?" He leaned past Cyrus, offered a hand to Lark. "Ms. Porter, good to see you again."

"I'm surprised you remember me," she responded, opening her door and climbing out of the car.

"I'm surprised you're back in this neck of the woods. Last time I saw you, you seemed bent on getting as far away from Amos Way as you could," he said. "You have any weapons on you, Mitchell?"

"A handgun."

"Permit to carry?"

"My boss has a copy."

"You're supposed to have that on you."

"It got confiscated. Maybe you could call your half brother and ask him to bring it to town."

Johnson scowled but didn't take the bait. "Remove the firearm, set it on the ground."

Cyrus did what he was asked. No way was he giving the guy an excuse to pull his service weapon.

He stepped back so Sheriff Johnson could take the Glock.

"This it?" Johnson asked, unloading the gun and shoving it in his pocket.

"I have a bowie knife strapped to my calf." He reached to unstrap it, heard the soft pop of a silenced gun, felt a bullet rip through his upper arm.

There was no pain, just the urgent need to protect Lark.

He dragged her to the ground, covering her body with his. He didn't know who had fired the shot, had no idea where it had come from, but he was certain the guy was gunning for him.

"Under the Mustang," he urged, shifting his weight so that Lark could roll out from under him.

"Stay down," Sheriff Johnson shouted, his

service weapon in hand. Another pop, and the pavement beside Cyrus's head exploded, bits of shrapnel hitting his back and neck.

The sheriff fired two shots in quick succession, the air vibrating with the force of the reports. Silence followed, the night thick with it.

"Stay here," Sheriff Johnson ordered, his boots pounding against the blacktop as he ran into the shrubs, his radio crackling as he called for backup. Had he hit his mark?

Cyrus shifted, blood dripping from his arm. He ignored it. He'd had worse injuries.

"You okay?" he asked, peering under the car. Lark lay flat under the center of the car, her face turned toward him, her eyes gleaming in the darkness.

"I'd be better if you were under here with me." She paused, probably realized how that sounded. "What I mean is, I'd be happier if we had both taken cover."

"I knew what you meant."

"So, maybe you should scoot under and stay out of sight until the sheriff returns."

"The shooter is gone." Or dead. He didn't mention that possibility, but it was a real one. The sheriff hadn't been shooting randomly. He'd aimed in the directions the bullets had come from, and he'd planned to hit his mark.

"Maybe."

"Probably," he corrected.

"Probably isn't for sure. Which means he could still be hanging around waiting to get a clear shot at you," she hissed, belly crawling toward him and grabbing his hand. "Get under here!"

"If he's going to take a shot, I'd rather it be aimed at me."

"Don't sacrifice yourself for me, Cyrus. I could never forgive myself if you did." She tried to pull him under the car, but she was probably seventy pounds lighter than him, and there was no way he was going to move until he wanted to.

"And Essex would never forgive me if I let something happen to you."

"I'm not Essex's responsibility, and I'm not yours. If something happens to me, it will be because I'm an idiot and stuck my hand in the viper's nest," she responded drily. "You're welcome to tell Essex that, if I die."

"You're not going to die." Not if he could help it, and he thought that he could. Once the team arrived, he wanted to get her into a safe house, keep her there until they could figure out exactly what was going on.

"It's clear," Sheriff Johnson called from somewhere beyond the hedges.

Cyrus stood, blood seeping from the gouge

in his upper arm. A flesh wound. Nothing he couldn't bandage up and treat himself. It could have been a lot worse, *would* have been a lot worse if he hadn't moved just as the perp pulled the trigger.

Lark scrambled out from under the car, got to her feet as the sheriff stepped into view.

He didn't look happy.

Shoulders slumped, gun holstered, he walked toward them. "Everyone okay over here?" he asked.

"I'll be better once I know that the perp has been apprehended," Cyrus replied, his pulse still racing with adrenaline.

"He's not going to be bothering you anymore," Johnson said grimly.

"He's dead?" Lark sounded surprised.

"Yes." Just one word, but Cyrus heard a boatload of emotion in it.

"You knew him, didn't you?" he asked.

"John McDermott and I went way back," he responded, opening the passenger door of the cruiser. "I'm not happy that he's dead, but I did what I had to. Why don't you have a seat until my deputies arrive, Lark? We'll go back to the station once they get here. I've called an ambulance, too. You look like you could use one, Mitchell."

"I'd rather have some information."

"About?" Johnson eyed him dispassionately, his expression unreadable. He had to know there were going to be questions. He had to know that his connection to Amos Way was going to come under scrutiny.

"Your connection to John."

"I don't owe you an explanation, but I'll give you one. I spent my senior year of high school in Amos Way. John and I were in the same class."

"You were friends?" he pressed, and Johnson shook his head.

"Not even close. The two of us didn't see eye to eye on things."

"What things?"

"I believe in abiding by the law of the land and in upholding it. He believes that the government needs to be shut down and that individuals should take over." He ran a hand down his jaw, frowned. "Believ*ed*."

It sounded good. Sounded like something that could be truth, but Cyrus knew nothing about Sheriff Johnson. It seemed very convenient that John was dead. He'd been the one who'd tied Lark up. He'd been the one who'd kept her prisoner in the trailer. With him dead, there was no one to press charges against and no way to prove that Elijah had condoned what had been done to Lark.

It was possible that was exactly the way Elijah wanted it. "How about Elijah?" he asked bluntly. "Do you see eye to eye with him?"

Johnson's jaw tightened, and he scowled. "No."

The answer was quick and just as blunt as the question had been.

"But you did live in the compound he runs for a year."

"Because my parents died. It was that or go into foster care. Not something I was interested in doing. But that's not something that I need to explain to you, Mitchell. Seems to me, you're the one who needs to explain. But first, how about you remove the knife from your calf?"

He did, because he knew he had no choice.

He set it on the ground, and the sheriff grabbed it, tossed it into the trunk of his cruiser. "Any other weapons?"

"A gun in the glove compartment," he responded, waiting impatiently while the sheriff retrieved it.

"How about you?" the sheriff asked, his attention on Lark. "Any weapons?"

"No."

"And you had a good reason to return to Amos Way?" he asked, and Lark shrugged.

"I'm not going to lie," she responded. "My in-laws invited me back to the compound. They wanted some pictures of Joshua, and I was happy to bring them. I'd actually been considering a trip back anyway, because—"

"You wanted to prove that your husband didn't accidentally kill himself," he cut her off. "You should have stayed away. Or called me before you decided to go out there. Things aren't what they seem in that community. Been trying to take the whole place down for a couple of years now."

That was an interesting piece of information.

Cyrus wanted to ask the sheriff to elaborate, but two cruisers rounded the corner of the building, speeding into the lot, lights flashing, sirens off. They parked a few yards away, an officer exiting each, their faces shadowed by uniform hats. One—a tall thin kid who looked like he'd just graduated high school—had his hand on his gun.

"You have everything under control, Sheriff?" he called.

"Yeah," Johnson responded, his eyes still focused on Lark. "You two stay here," he barked, then he strode over to meet his deputies.

John was dead.

Lark didn't know how to feel about that.

He'd been shooting at Cyrus. He'd obviously been trying to kill him, but she didn't want him dead. She wanted him to have a chance to repent, to tell the truth about what had happened to Joshua. He'd known. She was nearly certain of it. He was probably responsible for Joshua's death. Whether he'd pulled the trigger or hired someone else to do it, the results had been the same. Joshua had died, and his blood had been on John's hands.

"He got what he was asking for, Lark," Cyrus said as if he were reading her mind and knew exactly where her thoughts had gone.

"That won't make his death easier on his family," she responded. "He has a wife and three children."

"I know, and I'm sorry for them. But, John should have thought about what this would do to them before he decided to follow us into town." He touched her arm, urged her to take a seat in Sheriff Johnson's car. She sat because her legs were shaky and her head still hurt, and because she didn't think she could stay on her feet for another second.

"They're going to be devastated." Grace McDermott had always been shy and quiet, but she'd been kind, too. She'd bent over backward to make Lark feel comfortable in Amos Way.

Of course, when Lark returned, she'd avoided her like the plague. John's doing. He had iron-fisted control over his family and that included Grace, but Grace had loved him deeply, defended him staunchly.

"Don't carry their burdens, Lark. You have enough of your own to shoulder."

"I'm not shouldering anything."

He raised a dark brow, his eyes gleaming in the dim light.

"Okay," she conceded. "I'm not shouldering anyone else's burden. But I've been where John's wife is about to stand. I know what it's like to lose someone you love. My concern for John's family has nothing to do with carrying their burden and everything to do with knowing how it feels to stand in those shoes."

"I know it's difficult—"

"Saying it's difficult is like seeing a breathtakingly beautiful sunset and saying, *look, the sun is going down*," she snapped, because she hated that word. *Difficult* didn't begin to describe the anguish of losing a loved one. It didn't begin to express the depth of the heartache, the gaping wound that never quite healed.

"I'm sorry," he said, the apology simple and sincere. No excuses, no trying to backtrack and say something else. Just...*I'm sorry*, and she appreciated that more than all the thousands of platitudes she'd received after Joshua's death.

She swallowed down something that tasted

suspiciously like tears, blinked away the moisture in her eyes. "Thank you."

He nodded, his gaze never wavering, his focus so intense, she felt it like a physical touch.

"The thing about John," he finally said, and the moment was gone, that feeling that he was connecting with nothing more than a look, disappearing into the cool September air, "is that he knew what he was getting into when he came out here tonight, and he knew what was going to happen when he took those shots at me while the sheriff was nearby. He had to have weighed the risks and rewards very carefully."

"What rewards? Your death? Because I can't see what he'd have to gain from that."

"My silence, Lark. I was in the compound long enough to notice some things that he might not have wanted me to talk about."

"The deliveries and shipments?"

"Right. The storage sheds are locked up tighter than Fort Knox. Whatever it is they're bringing into the compound, it's valuable."

"It's not worth a human life," she replied. Or three. John was dead. Joshua was dead. Ethan was probably dead. She shuddered.

"Cold?" he asked.

"Tired. Confused. John didn't have to die. He could have gone back to the compound, packed up and left."

"People do desperate things when they're desperate," he said, fingering the edges of the wound in his upper arm. It had stopped bleeding, but blood stained a wide swatch of fabric around the area, his white shirt soaked with it. "And maybe John forgot that blindly following orders doesn't always end well."

"Elijah wanted you dead and me alive? Is that what you think?"

"I don't think it. I know it. You have something Elijah wants, and I have information he wants to keep secret."

"What information?" Had he found out the truth about what Amos Way was hiding? If so, he'd done what she hadn't been able to.

"That you were kept against your will. That Elijah knew about it. If I'd died, it would have been your word against theirs. With me still around, it's going to be a little harder to pretend that you've made everything up." His gaze shifted, his attention focused on Sheriff Johnson and his men. "It'll be interesting to see what the sheriff does with that."

"He said he was trying to bring down Amos Way."

"People say all kinds of things, Lark. That doesn't mean they're true."

She had firsthand knowledge of that.

She'd been lied to plenty when she was a kid.

Her mother had made a million promises and never followed through. She'd told hundreds of lies to cover her addictions. Things had been different with Joshua. He'd been honest, shared everything, kept his promises.

Until the end.

Then, he'd been secretive. He'd been quiet.

She frowned, pressing a finger to her brow, trying to ease the pain there. Joshua had been digging around. He'd been convinced that Ethan had disappeared because he'd rocked the boat, asked Elijah for proof that he was using community funds for community expenses. Joshua had told Lark that, and then he hadn't told her anything. He'd slip out late at night, come back before the sun rose. She'd tried to follow him once, and he'd threatened to bring her back to Baltimore and leave her there.

It was too dangerous, he'd said.

But he'd continued to look for evidence, continued to dig around.

If he'd found anything, he hadn't told her. As a matter of fact, those last few months were the only time in their marriage when she hadn't felt connected to him, deeply in love with him, absolutely certain that they were meant to be together forever. His silence had filled the house they'd shared with his family, it had filled their bedroom, their times together.

She'd asked him, begged him, pleaded with him, but he refused to tell her what was going on. A season, she'd thought. A little blip on the radar of their lives together. It would be over once he found what he was looking for, and they'd go on with their lives, create something wonderful again.

Only it hadn't happened that way.

He'd died before they could reconnect, and she'd been left alone.

"You okay?" Cyrus asked, touching her shoulder, his palm warm and oddly comforting.

She wasn't okay, hadn't been okay for a long time, but she couldn't tell him that, barely wanted to admit it to herself. "Fine. Just..."

"What?" His eyes were black in the dim light, the shadow of a beard darkening his jaw. He had a hard look, a tough one, but his hand was gentle as it kneaded the tense muscles in her shoulder.

"You need to get that arm looked at." She jumped up too quickly, and the world shifted, the night going blacker than brighter, silent than loud.

She'd never passed out before. Ever.

But she thought she might, and she grabbed the closest thing to her, her hands gripping crisp cotton and firm muscles.

"I think you're the one who needs to be

looked at," Cyrus muttered as he scooped her into his arms.

She wanted to protest, but the words wouldn't form. Nothing seemed to be working. Not her brain, not her muscles, not her ears.

People were talking, but the words seemed to bounce in and out, unclear and unintelligible.

Sirens screamed. Lights flashed.

She was moving, flying along bumpy pavement strapped to a gurney. Then, she was in an ambulance, a medic leaning over her.

"You're going to be fine," he said.

But she wasn't sure she would be, because the world was fading to black, the screaming siren fading to silence, and she was alone. Just exactly the way she had been the day Joshua died.

NINE

"You got what you deserved," Stella said as an ER doctor carefully stitched Cyrus's arm.

Too carefully.

He wanted to take the needle and thread and do it himself. He figured he'd be a lot faster, and fast was what he wanted. That and free access to the triage room where they were treating Lark.

"I guess you have a reason for saying that," he growled, and Stella looked up from the text she'd been reading and sighed.

"Really, Cyrus? You're going to play that card?"

"What card?" He wasn't in the mood for twenty questions. He wasn't in the mood for lectures. Radley Johnson was interviewing Lark while she was being treated, and he wanted to be there.

"The clueless card," Stella responded. She had dark circles under her eyes, and a purple scar under her chin that ran from one side to the other. Seeing it made him soften. He liked Stella. She was a consummate professional, and a huge asset to the team. She'd taken some hits recently, though, had nearly lost her life on her last mission. She'd been recovering for nearly three months, had just recently returned to work.

As far as he knew, this was the first job she'd taken since she'd been released from the hospital.

"You look tired," he said, and she scowled.

"Don't try to change the subject, Cyrus. You should have had someone else go into the compound with you. If we'd done the married-couple-looking-for-religious-nirvana thing like I suggested, you wouldn't be getting your arm stitched up."

"You're making an assumption that may or may not be true."

"It's true, because if I'd been with you, I would have made sure you didn't do anything stupid." She typed something into her phone, her fingers flying, the scar on her right wrist darker and thicker than the one on her chin. They'd been betrayed in Somalia, and she'd taken the brunt of that, the kidnappers who'd been holding a diplomat's son determined to use her as an example to anyone else who might be tempted to go against them.

Only Stella was tougher than she looked, more determined to live than they'd imagined. He wanted to ask her if she was okay, but she'd have taken his head off.

"I didn't do anything stupid," he said instead.

"And yet, you've got a ten-inch slice in your upper arm. In a situation like the one you were in, backup would have been invaluable."

"Is this your version of *I told you so*?"

"It's my version of me not being happy that you're in the hospital. Again."

"Visiting a hospital to get stitches isn't the same as being admitted and staying for a week," he pointed out.

"And that makes it all better?" She stood, stretching to her full height. Which wasn't all that tall, but Stella filled space like nobody's business when she was upset. "I told you this mission wasn't going to be as easy as you thought it would be. If you'd listened—"

"You and Chance wouldn't have had the opportunity to take a three-and-a-half-hour drive together."

She scowled, her eyes flashing with irritation. Chance Miller hadn't mentioned his plan to come to River Fork. Not while he'd been talking to Cyrus. It could have been that he was concerned about having his team step on toes in small-town America. Getting a bad reputation was a surefire way to close down a business, and HEART was Chance's baby, his brainchild. He'd conceived of the idea, built the hostage rescue team from the ground up, handpicking the men and women who worked for him.

Cyrus had a feeling there was another reason that Chance had made the trip. Stella hadn't been herself since she'd returned from Somalia, and Chance had made no secret of the fact that he was worried about her.

"Do not mention that man's name to me again," she snapped, shoving her phone into the pocket of her navy-colored coat.

"He's your boss." Also her ex-boyfriend, but he decided not to mention that. "I think you're going to hear his name a lot."

"Not in the next ten minutes," she responded, moving closer and watching as the doctor put in the last stitch. "Unless Boone comes walking in here spouting off about what that man wants us to do next."

"You know, Stella," Cyrus said as the doctor bandaged his arm. "If I didn't know better, I'd think you were still smitten with Cha—"

"I don't do smitten," she cut him off.

"You must. You were married." And widowed before Cyrus had ever met her. He didn't know much of the story, but he knew that she'd loved her husband, and that everyone on the team had been surprised when she and Chance had started spending time together.

"I wasn't smitten with Gus. I loved him."

"There's a difference?" he asked.

"Smitten is what you have before you really know someone. Love is what happens when you know a person—every wart and every wound—and you love him anyway," she said, pulling open the triage room door. "Obviously, you're going to live. I'm going to get some coffee."

She stalked from the room, and he stood.

The ER doctor sat in front of a computer, typing something. Whatever it was, Cyrus didn't have time for it. "Thanks for stitching me up," he said, walking to the door.

"It's my job," the doctor said, not bothering to look up from the screen. "But I appreciate the thanks."

Cyrus stepped out into the hall, and the doctor finally looked up.

"Hold on," he called. "I'm going to print out your discharge instructions. That was a pretty deep wound. You need to check in with your doctor within the next couple of days."

"I'll do that. Thanks."

"Let me print this out before you go. It will

only take a couple of minutes," the doctor said, apparently confused by Cyrus's rush to leave.

"I need to check on my friend. I'll pick the paperwork up at the front desk."

"If you're talking about Lark Porter, she's already been released," the doctor said absently as he turned his attention back to the computer and began typing again.

The news sent a shot of adrenaline through Cyrus.

"When?"

"I handed her follow-up instructions right before I came in here to stitch you up."

That explained the text Stella had been reading. Either Boone or Chance had given her information that no one had bothered giving Cyrus. They'd probably been afraid he'd walk out of the hospital before the doctor was finished stitching him up if he knew that they were leaving with Lark.

They were right.

He would have, but that was his decision to make. Not theirs.

He stalked into the hall, walked out of the triage area. No sign of Stella in the waiting room, but the receptionist was happy to point him toward the hospital's cafeteria.

Stella was there, sitting at a booth in a far corner of the room, staring into a cup of coffee.

She looked…sad. Which surprised Cyrus. Usually, she was filled with sharp wit and offering sharp retorts, her expression waxing and waning between exasperation and intense concentration.

She didn't look up as he approached, and he thought that she hadn't noticed him, hadn't realized he was moving toward her.

He should have known better.

"So, you're done," she said, still staring into the coffee cup.

"And you're keeping secrets."

"No secrets, Cyrus. Just information that I planned to disseminate at an appropriate time." She stood, finally meeting his eyes. The sadness was gone, and she looked like she always did—just a little hot under the collar.

"I don't need you to protect me."

"I'm not protecting you. I'm protecting Lark. That's what we're here for, and you running out of the hospital with a wide-open wound on your gun arm isn't going to benefit the team, and that's not going to benefit her."

"Where are they headed?" he asked, dropping the subject, because neither of them would win the debate. She had her way of doing things. He had his. They still always managed to work well together.

"Over to the sheriff's department. I have

directions. Johnson wants to take your statement while we're there. Once he's done that, we should be free to go."

"Any information on how Johnson is going to handle things?"

"He's not going to bust down the gate at Amos Way and arrest Elijah Clayton, if that's what you're asking," she responded, leading the way out of the cafeteria. "The way the boss tells it, Johnson is trying to procure a search warrant for the compound. With Lark's testimony about being held prisoner there, he should be able to get the local judge to issue one. Once he arrives at work. Which, apparently, won't be until sometime Monday morning."

"You're kidding, right?" Anything could happen in that amount of time. Certainly whatever had been hidden in those storage sheds would be gone before then.

"I wish I were, but this is very small-town America. The town has four full-time police officers, six part-time and one judge."

"You've been doing your research."

"The boss did the research. I'm just spouting what he found out for you."

"The boss, huh?"

"Yeah. The *boss*. Now, hurry it up, Cyrus," she demanded as she held open the exit door.

"The sooner we get this over with, the sooner we can head home and I get can some sleep."

"I guess I was right about you being tired."

"I passed tired six hours ago, but we just keep going, right?" She smiled, but it didn't meet her eyes, didn't make her look any less exhausted than she was. "Now, move! I'm getting impatient."

"Getting?" he responded as he walked outside into cool dawn. The first rays of sunlight splashed across the sky in an array of gold and pink that glinted off distant mountains and set fire to the orange-and-red foliage.

If he'd been home, he'd have gone camping on a weekend like this, spent a few days outdoors, clearing his head, trying to find his center and his balance.

Life had been crazy the past few years. One mission after another. One trip after another. He didn't have a family, didn't have the kind of relationships that required plenty of time and attention, so he was often chosen for the missions that required long amounts of time out of the country. Sometimes weeks. Sometimes months. During those times, he'd be deep undercover, working an angle to get to whomever it was HEART had been paid to rescue. That was the way he'd wanted it.

There were times, though, when he wanted

to be home. Times when he wanted all that home should mean—people waiting for his return, smiles and conversations and even arguments. He had a nice apartment in a nice neighborhood. He had friends and, recently, a church that he attended when he was in town.

What he didn't have was what two of the HEART team members had found. Jackson and Boone had both found women who understood their schedules, who supported their goals. They'd found that special kind of peace that only came when a person was exactly where he was supposed to be.

Even out in the woods, even with nature all around him, God's creation nearly shouting the truth of God's power, Cyrus didn't have that.

Maybe. One day.

When he wasn't so busy that he barely had time to breathe let alone think.

He got into Stella's SUV, took a small bag she handed him. He opened it, smiled. Inside were the things he'd left behind when he'd exchanged his real identity for his assumed one. His wallet. His phone. No more Louis Morgan. He was officially Cyrus Mitchell again.

"I picked them up from the office," she said.

He shoved his wallet into his pocket, grabbed his phone. Fully charged. Of course. Stella wasn't the kind of person who let any details go. "Thanks."

"Thank me by making your statement to the sheriff short and concise," she responded, speeding onto the road.

He didn't tell her to slow down.

He was just as anxious to get to the sheriff's department as she was.

She wanted out, but she didn't think Sheriff Johnson would appreciate her climbing out his office window and scrambling down the fire escape. Lark also didn't think he was going to let her waltz out of the office, down the three flights of stairs and out the door.

She paced across the small office, looked out the third-floor window for what seemed like the thousandth time. It didn't change anything. She was still in Sheriff Johnson's office, waiting. He'd assured her that he'd be back shortly. That had been thirty minutes ago.

Thirty very long minutes.

At least her head wasn't pounding anymore, and she had on a fresh set of clothes. Soft jeans that were a little too long and a little too big. Faded blue T-shirt that was just as soft and comfortable as the jeans. One of Cyrus's coworkers had handed them to her, and she'd been so excited to have them that she hadn't asked where they'd come from.

Probably Stella Silverstone's. Lark had met her briefly when the HEART team had arrived at the hospital. Chance Miller, Boone Anderson and Stella. They'd been kind, but all business, asking questions rapidly and purposefully. They knew what they were doing. She'd had that impression. She'd also thought they were a good team, all of them in sync and working toward a common goal.

That goal seemed to be getting Cyrus back to their headquarters in Washington, DC, and keeping Lark safe.

She wanted those things, but she also wanted Elijah taken down. She wanted Amos Way closed. She wanted the people who lived there—the ones who really believed the lie, who had no idea that Elijah was running something more than a religious community—to find something better, something more real, something truer than the lie they'd been fed.

She opened the office door, peered out into the hallway, determined to find the sheriff and find out exactly what was going on. A few feet away, a tall red-haired man leaned against the wall, what looked like a doughnut in his hand.

"Hungry?" he asked, gesturing to a white box that sat on a chair someone had pushed up against the wall. "There's ten more where this one came from."

"No. Thank you, Mr. Anderson."

"Boone. That's what my friends call me. It's what my clients call me. It's what my wife calls me. As a matter of fact," he said, taking another doughnut from the box, "it's what everyone calls me."

"I'll keep that in mind," she responded, stepping out into the hall and trying to remember if the staircase was to the left or the right.

"You going somewhere?" Boone asked conversationally. He seemed more focused on the doughnut than on her.

"I was looking for Sheriff Johnson. I'm curious to hear what he plans to do about Elijah and Amos Way."

"Aren't we all?" Boone licked chocolate off his finger and eyed the box. "I'm thinking about having another one. I'm also thinking that you need to go back in the office."

"I've been there for thirty minutes. I need the change of scenery."

"Do you need a bullet through the heart, ma'am?" he asked. "Because that's what might happen if you wander around on your own."

The words were enough to make her pause. "John is dead."

"And Elijah is alive, and so are most of his

security team. For all we know, there's a price on your head."

She hadn't thought about that.

She probably should have.

Elijah had enough money to get the things he wanted. Even if what he wanted was someone dead. "He'd be a fool to hire a hit man," she said. "If the police catch the guy, he's going to point his finger straight at Elijah."

"Will that matter if you're dead?" Boone asked as he opened the doughnut box.

"I don't guess that it would," she murmured, suddenly not nearly as comfortable with her plan as she had been.

"I agree," he said with a charming smile. "Now, go on back into the office. Take a load off your feet, and give the sheriff a few more minutes. He'll be back before you know it."

He cupped her elbow, urged her over the threshold and into the office.

Next thing she knew, the door was closing in her face, and she was right back where she started.

Trapped.

The guy was smooth. She'd give him that. But she still had no intention of waiting another minute. She was in a police station. Even if Sheriff Johnson was on his brother's payroll, she couldn't imagine that he'd try to murder her there.

"He'd be shot by his own police force if he did," she muttered, yanking the door open and walking straight into a hard chest.

She jumped back, her heart slamming against her ribs as she looked into Cyrus's dark brown eyes. "Cyrus!"

"You were expecting someone else?" he said. He had a full-out five-o'clock shadow, and the sleeve of his shirt had been cut off to the shoulder, a bandage wrapped around his biceps.

"The sheriff," she admitted. "But I'm just as happy to see you."

Boone snorted.

"We're not interested in hearing from the peanut gallery, Boone," Cyrus said, and Boone laughed.

"I'll keep that in mind."

"I won't hold my breath on that." Cyrus's gaze drifted back to Lark, and he offered her a smile that made her heart do a funny little dance. "How are you feeling?"

"I'm not the one who was shot."

"Grazed by a bullet," he corrected. "Which is not the same thing. So…how *are* you feeling?"

"Much better. How about you?"

"Like he's been ridden hard and put up wet,

would be my guess," Boone intoned, and Cyrus shot him a hard look.

"How about you shove another one of those doughnuts in your mouth?"

"You've wounded me, Cyrus, but—" he reached into the box, took another doughnut "—don't mind if I do."

There was something about him that made Lark smile, and she was still smiling when Cyrus took her hand, led her back into the sheriff's office.

A few minutes ago, she'd been anxious to escape. Now, the room didn't seem as small, her need to leave didn't seem nearly as desperate.

"How are you? Really?" she asked as Cyrus pulled a chair away from Sheriff Johnson's desk and gestured for her to sit.

"Like I've been ridden hard and put up wet."

His response surprised a laugh out of her.

"There you go," he said. "That's better."

"Better than what?"

"Better than you looking scared to death."

"I *am* scared to death," she said truthfully, because he was watching her with those deep brown eyes, his expression intense and soft all at the same time.

"You're safe here."

"I'm not scared for my safety. I'm scared for all the people who are still living in Amos Way.

I'm afraid that they'll go another thirty years with Elijah as their leader. That whatever he's doing will never be uncovered. That—"

"That's a lot of worries, Lark." He cut her off. "But none of them are yours to carry."

"You're wrong. I lived in Amos Way for three years. I got to know the people there. A lot of them were wonderful, warm and caring, and they deserve better than what they're getting."

"That doesn't mean that it's your responsibility to make things better for them."

"Someone has to do it."

"Someone isn't going to be you. We're heading back to Maryland tonight. I already spoke with Sheriff Johnson. He agreed to allow it as long as he has our contact information."

Go back to Maryland?

It sounded like a great plan, a wonderful one. Probably the best plan she'd heard of in a long time.

But she didn't know if she could do it.

She hadn't proven anything. Bringing Elijah down wouldn't raise Joshua from the dead, but it would make the memories a little easier to live with. "I'm not going back."

His eyes narrowed. "You're not thinking that you can stay in River Fork?"

There were tiny lines fanning out from the corners of his eyes, a small scar near his ear. He looked like he spent a lot of time out in the sun, and like he was used to getting what he wanted.

This time, he was going to be disappointed.

"That's exactly what I'm thinking. People around here have probably seen things, heard things. They probably know things that they won't just come out and say. They need to be asked."

"And you don't need to be the one to do the asking."

"My husband is dead. He shouldn't be," she responded. "I can't go home until I know why."

His jaw tightened, and she had a feeling they were in for a rip-roaring debate.

They probably would have had one, but the office door opened, and Sheriff Johnson walked in. A man stood behind him, a cardboard box in his hands. Tall, a little stooped in the shoulders, a white beard covering the lower half of his face. Blue eyes that should have been kind, but always seemed cold.

Elijah Clayton.

He walked into the room, his gaze settling on Lark.

For a moment, he said nothing. Did nothing.

And then he smiled, the kind of smile that said he was still in control, the kind that said he knew exactly what she'd been trying to do, and that he was going to make sure she failed.

"My dear," he murmured, walking toward her, that smile still fixed in place, those eyes still cold. "I've been so worried about you."

"You have a funny way of showing it," she responded, barely managing to get to her feet, to stand in front of him without cowering.

"I had no idea that John had you locked in the trailer. I thought you were there of your own accord. Meditating and praying about your future." He continued as if she hadn't spoken. "You must know that I would never be part of what he did. As much as we will all mourn John's death, it's better this way. The community would have had to exile him, and that would have been painful for everyone."

"It's great that you're so concerned about other people," Cyrus cut in, his arm settling around Lark's waist—a silent show of support that she needed more than she wanted to. "Too bad you weren't concerned when Lark was trussed up, lying in filth on that old trailer floor."

Elijah's eyes flashed. "You are a liar. A man ruled by the dark—"

"Enough," Sheriff Johnson said quietly. "You said you had some things to return to Lark. I'm giving you that opportunity."

"Yes. Of course." Elijah smiled again. "I brought your car keys, your phone. All the things you turned in when you entered the compound. And this."

He lifted something from the box. A small envelope splattered with dark red drops.

Blood?

Ice ran through her veins, and she tried to back up, didn't want to take what he was offering.

"It's for you," Elijah said. "John removed it from the scene of Joshua's accident before the police arrived. You were distraught, of course, and didn't notice it lying on the table."

He held it out, but she didn't take it, was afraid of what it might be.

"Go ahead." He thrust it toward her, his eyes alive with something that looked like glee. "Take it. John and I wanted to protect you and Joshua's family, but Radley says you want the truth. That's it. Right there in your husband's hand."

She took it, her fingers numb, her body numb as she saw her name scrawled across the front. The writing was Joshua's. She recognized the curve of the *L*, the little heart he'd always used for the *A*.

"Open it," Elijah urged, and she turned the envelope, lifted the flap, felt Cyrus's hand tighten on her waist as she pulled a lone piece of paper out.

TEN

"I love you. I'm sorry."

Black words on white paper that had been stained with blood. Cyrus knew that's what it was. He wasn't sure that Lark did.

She turned the paper over, her hand steady, her breathing even. Whatever she was feeling, she wasn't going to give Elijah the satisfaction of seeing her reaction to the note.

He was glad.

The man was a charlatan, and he needed to be ousted from his position of power.

"Well?" Elijah demanded, his voice booming into the silence.

"He didn't kill himself," Lark said, sliding the note back into the envelope and putting it in the box.

"That note says different," Elijah snapped. "I would have given it to you weeks ago, if you'd been honest about why you'd returned to Amos Way."

"Like you've been honest about what you're doing in the compound?" Cyrus demanded, and Elijah turned toward him, eyes blazing with the kind of zeal usually associated with delusional fanatics. Cyrus had thought Elijah to be a schemer, a fake, a man who was using people to gain wealth, who had become a religious leader to exert whatever flimsy control he could.

Maybe he'd been wrong.

Maybe the guy was nuts.

"I," Elijah spat, "do not need to answer to you. My God is my judge. He is my—"

"I think it's time for you to go, Elijah," Sheriff Johnson said wearily.

"You're kicking me out of your office? After I took you in? Tried to get you on the right path. Tried to teach you God's—"

"I'm kicking you out. I suggest that you stay away from Lark. No contact at all."

"I do not force my ideals and faith on others." Elijah seemed to have reeled himself in, gotten his emotions under control.

"This isn't about your faith," Lark said, her gaze on the box and the envelope that was in it. "It's about truth. I'm going to find it, Elijah. I'm not going to stop until I do."

Elijah stiffened, his shoulders straightening

beneath the crisp white tunic he always wore. "May God's will will be done."

"You don't know God," Lark continued, and Cyrus would have told her not to yank the tail of a rattler, but she had a right to speak her mind. She needed to speak it, and this was the safest place to do it. "If you did, Joshua would still be alive. Ethan would be alive. There are probably others. People who are buried in the woods somewhere, dead because you know nothing about love and everything about selfishness and greed."

Elijah moved so fast that Cyrus barely had time to react. He just managed to snag the man's wrist before his hand hit Lark's cheek.

"That," Cyrus growled, twisting Elijah's arm up behind his back, "was a mistake."

"Trouble?" Boone asked from the doorway.

"Nothing that I can't handle."

"I'll handle it," Sheriff Johnson said, his tone flat. "Let him go."

Cyrus hesitated.

What he wanted to do was teach Elijah a lesson he wouldn't forget.

But getting himself arrested wasn't going to do Lark any good.

He let Elijah go, positioning himself between him and Lark.

"You go home, Elijah," Sheriff Johnson

barked. "Stay home, because I'm going to be paying you a visit. We're going to have a long talk about what's going on in Amos Way, and I'm going to want some answers."

"You're not welcome on my property, Radley. Not anymore. Not since you betrayed the faith." Elijah pivoted sharply, shoved past Boone and disappeared.

"Well," Boone said. "That was fun."

"Not from where I was standing," Sheriff Johnson growled. He reached into the box, pulled out the envelope. "Do you mind if I take a look, Lark?"

She shrugged, stepping around Cyrus and heading toward the door.

Boone blocked her path, doing exactly what Cyrus knew he'd been told to do—keep her in place, make sure she didn't disappear again.

"I need some air," she said.

Boone met Cyrus's eyes, and Cyrus nodded. He'd follow her, make sure she didn't find her way into more trouble.

He walked down the hall a few steps behind her, followed her into the stairwell and down a flight of steps. She paused on the landing, glancing over her shoulder, her eyes misty gray. "I don't want to talk."

"Okay."

"And I know what was on the envelope and letter."

"Okay," he repeated as he stepped onto the landing. Lark had changed into jeans and a T-shirt that Stella had pulled from her overnight bag. The jeans were loose and long, the T-shirt hugging slender curves. She was even smaller than she'd seemed when she'd been wearing the long skirt and sweater, her collarbones jutting out of the V neck, her upper arms muscular and lean.

"It's probably his blood," she said as if she hadn't heard him, as if she were working through what she'd just seen, figuring it all out.

"Maybe." Maybe not. Elijah was trying to cover his tail, and he'd do anything, fabricate anything to keep the police from entering the compound and conducting a thorough search. It was too late for that, but Elijah didn't know it. That was going to work out well for Sheriff Johnson. If he wasn't working behind the scenes to help his brother.

Lark sighed, easing down onto the step, wrapping her arms around her knees. She looked vulnerable and sad, her expression so open, so filled with anguish, that he sat beside her, tugged her close, his arm around her waist, his fingers caressing her side.

He meant to comfort her, but when she

leaned into him, when her head rested against his shoulder, he felt an odd sense of rightness, of certainty. As if he were, for just that moment, exactly where he was supposed to be, doing exactly what he should be doing.

"He didn't kill himself," Lark said so quietly he almost didn't hear. "He wouldn't have. But that was his writing on the envelope. He always put a heart where the *A* was." Her voice broke, and he wanted to go down the stairs, find Elijah and shake the truth out of him.

"Writing styles can be copied," he said, but she shook her head.

"He had a unique way of writing my name. I'd recognize it anywhere." Her eyes were dry, but her voice sounded thick as if she were struggling to hold back tears.

"He could have been forced to write it."

She shook her head. "If he were going to die anyway, he wouldn't have given in to the request. He'd have refused, because he wouldn't want me to think he'd purposely left me."

"It sounds like he was a good guy."

"He was." She offered a shaky smile. "He was so…kind and funny. Everyone loved him, and he loved everyone. Including the people in Amos Way. Even after going to college and realizing that some of Elijah's doctrine was false, he still loved the place. He liked the idea of living a simpler life."

"There's nothing wrong with that," he said.

"No, I guess not, but it's what got him killed." She eased away from his arm, stood.

"Do you think Joshua suspected the truth about Elijah?" he asked.

"I know he did. By the time he died, Joshua and I were looking forward to leaving Amos Way. Joshua had a lot of integrity, though. Once he started suspecting that Elijah was hiding something, he couldn't just walk away and let things go. He wanted to find out the truth."

"Do you think he found it before he died?"

"I don't know." She tucked a strand of deep red hair behind her ear, fidgeted with the hem of her shirt. "He wasn't saying much the last couple of weeks. It was the first time in our marriage that I had to wonder what he was thinking. That plays with my mind if I let it. I start wondering if all the good things we had were my imagination, if maybe that last month was the truth about our relationship. All the silences, all the secrecy, maybe they were glimmers of a problem I didn't want to admit."

"He was trying to protect you, Lark," Cyrus said. He'd never met the guy, but it's what he would have done in Joshua's place.

"Maybe so. He's not here to tell me one way

or another." She sighed, looked up toward the third-floor landing. "I guess I'm going to have to go back."

"Not if you don't want to."

"You'd sneak me out?" she asked with a grin, some of the sorrow gone from her face and her eyes.

"I'd walk you out in full view of anyone who cared to see. You're not a prisoner, Lark. You haven't done anything wrong. If you want to leave, you can." As long as Cyrus and the team were with her. He decided not to add that. Lark had been through enough. He'd get her through this. Then, he'd try to get her to see just how much danger she was still in.

"Good to know, but I can't just walk out and go back to my life. Elijah still hasn't gotten what he wants from me, and I don't think he's going to give up trying for it. I want to look in that box he brought. See what he packed in it. I know Joshua was really digging around that last month. He discovered something. Maybe he hid the information somewhere."

"Did you bring everything of Joshua's back to the compound?"

"No. There wasn't much, and I didn't want to give all of it to my in-laws."

"Is that what they wanted?"

"I don't know." She headed back up the stairs.

"They asked for some photos." She frowned, a small line etching itself into her brow. "Actually, now that I think about it, they asked for photos and any mementos that I had. It struck me as odd, because photos are frowned upon in Amos Way. So are knickknacks and keepsakes."

"Did you question them?"

"Not really. My father-in-law said that Elijah had given them special permission to keep some of Joshua's things. Since I'd been thinking about going back to the compound, I let it go."

"Your father-in-law is Eric Porter?"

"Right."

He'd met the guy, hadn't gotten much out of him. He hadn't been allowed to speak with Maria Porter, Eric's wife. She'd stayed inside their home unless she was at church or prayer meeting. He'd gotten the impression that Eric called the shots and she was just along for the ride. "I spoke with him a couple of times. He didn't have a lot to say."

"He never does. Even when Joshua and I lived in my in-laws' house, Eric didn't say a whole lot to me." She slowed as she neared Sheriff Johnson's office, her feet dragging.

"You don't have to do this, Lark."

"You're right. I don't. I could run, but then I'd

just have to keep running. And you know what, Cyrus? All the running in the world couldn't put any distance between me and my memories."

She walked into the office without another word.

He followed, struck by her determination, by her strength. He'd rescued her from the compound because he'd owed Essex. Things were changing, though. It was becoming less about repaying his debt to Essex and more about Lark.

That could be a problem if he let it be.

Minimal emotional involvement had been his motto since Megan's death.

He hadn't planned to change that, didn't really want to change it, but he thought that maybe he was about to.

It didn't take long for Lark to go through the box.

She sat at the sheriff's desk, pulling out one item after the other. Elijah had packed everything she'd brought into the compound. Her street clothes folded neatly at the bottom of the box. The wedding photo. A few pictures that had been taken while she and Joshua were dating.

She lifted one, looking at Joshua's smiling

face and then her own. They'd been so happy, so filled with hope.

They'd had no idea what life was going to bring.

"What do you think?" Sheriff Johnson asked. "Is everything there?"

"Yes." She lifted the envelope that he'd left on his desk, studied the handwriting. She could imagine Joshua leaning over the page, looping that *L*, making the heart. Had he written the note inside?

She slid it out, held it carefully, not wanting to touch the drops of blood that had seeped through the envelope and stained the page.

Joshua's blood.

Thinking about it made her heart pound and her ears buzz.

She wasn't going to pass out, but she almost wanted to.

Anything to stop thinking about Joshua's last moments, to stop seeing his body lying on the floor, blood seeping out from under it.

She shivered, and someone dropped a coat onto her shoulders. Not Cyrus, he was standing at her elbow, so close his knee touched her leg.

She could have shifted away.

She didn't.

There hadn't been much that had comforted her in the days after Joshua's death. People in the compound had tried. Eric and Maria had tried. When she'd returned to Baltimore, old friends had come to visit. They'd offered condolences and distraction, but no one had been able to give her what she'd needed—a sense of comfort, a feeling that everything was going to be okay.

She'd had her faith. She'd had God. It had been enough, but there had been nights when she'd lain in bed crying for something more. What she'd wanted, what she'd needed more than anything else was to not feel so alone.

Cyrus had sat on the steps with her. He'd put his arm around her, and for just a moment, she'd felt comfort and a sense of belonging that had died with Joshua.

She didn't want to let that go even though she knew she should.

Her hand shook, so she laid the paper on the desk, read it a dozen times as if rereading it could change the words.

"I love you. I'm sorry."

Just five words. Not enough to leave for someone you loved.

"The *L* is different," Cyrus said, leaning down to get a closer look, his bandaged arm brushing her cheek.

"What?" Sheriff Johnson asked.

"Lark said her husband always wrote *L*s the

same way." He lifted the envelope, pointed to the looped *L*.

He was right, and Lark's pulse jumped at the knowledge.

She grabbed the letter, studied it more carefully. The L *was* different. Curved but without the loop. "He didn't write this."

"If he didn't, someone else did," the sheriff said grimly.

"I guess Lark's idea about her husband being murdered wasn't so far-fetched after all," Boone said.

Sheriff Johnson frowned, lifting the envelope, studying it intently. "I'm going to take this in for evidence, Lark. I want to see if the blood matches your husband's. If it does, this was written the day he died. If it doesn't, Elijah fabricated it later. I wouldn't put it past him."

"Either way," Cyrus responded before Lark could. "The letter is evidence that the shooting wasn't accidental."

"That's the way I'm seeing it," Sheriff Johnson admitted. "We're trying to push the search warrant through quickly. I want to get on the compound before my brother has a chance to clean things up."

"Clean what things?" Lark stood, her body stiff, her muscles tense. She felt a thousand years old. She'd suspected that Joshua had been murdered, but seeing that letter, the blood, the curly loop of his writing, it made it so much more real, the accusation so much more awful.

"Those storage sheds for one. I'd like to know what he has delivered and what he's shipping out."

"You know about that?" Cyrus asked, lifting the coat from Lark's shoulders, urging her to slip her arms into the sleeves.

"I've been keeping tabs on my brother for years. If I had probable cause that they were committing crimes on the compound, I'd have been in there searching two years ago. I don't know what my brother is up to, but it's bound to be trouble. And not just for people living in this county. Elijah thinks big. It's one of his greatest strengths and his biggest weaknesses."

"You going to send that letter in to the county? Or are you planning to process it here?" Boone asked.

"I'm sending it to the state. The county doesn't have a forensic evidence team, and I don't want anything missed."

It sounded good. Great even.

Lark should have been elated. She just felt… tired.

Cyrus zipped the coat. It fell to her knees, completely covered her hands. She shoved the sleeves up, tried to think of something to say.

All three men were watching her expectantly, but all she could think about was Joshua's last moments. Had he been afraid? Resigned? Had he seen the gunman? Or had he been surprised?

She turned blindly, ran out of the office, pounded down the steps. This time, she didn't stop at the landing, didn't sit and wait for Cyrus to catch up.

She made it to the lobby, saw Stella and Chance sitting in chairs near the door. She didn't say a word to either of them as she raced outside, gulped crisp morning air.

The sun had risen above the tree line, but clouds edged in on the horizon, a soft breeze carrying a hint of rain with it.

Joshua had loved the rain.

He'd loved the sun.

He'd loved the outdoors.

He'd been one of those people who always found something positive to say, who'd enjoyed life because he'd thought it was meant to be enjoyed. A gift. That's what he would have said.

She knew Cyrus had followed her outside. Figured that Stella and Boone and Chance were there, too. She didn't look over her shoulder, just kept her gaze on the horizon, kept her breathing even and deep.

Life happened. Good and bad and everything in between. She could mourn forever or she could move on. She'd chosen the second option, because it's what Joshua would have wanted. But it was so much harder than she ever could have imagined it would be.

"Running outside isn't the best idea you've ever had, Lark," Cyrus said, his breath ruffling her hair as he urged her around, looked into her face. "How about you don't do it again?"

"How about we just go?" she responded.

"Stella is pulling the car around. Sheriff Johnson is going to call as soon as he gets the search warrant. In the meantime, he thinks it's better if we take you to the safe house."

Safe house?

That was the first she'd heard of it.

"I don't need to be in a safe house, Cyrus. I need to be home."

"We're going to stop there first. I'd like to see the rest of Joshua's things. Maybe there's something hidden in them."

"A secret message?" It would have been just like Joshua to leave one. He'd loved cryptology, had spent most of his childhood making up secret codes that his friends would try to break. "That sounds like something Joshua would do."

"Yeah?" he sounded distracted, his eyes tracking the movement of every car that entered the lot. Behind him, Chance and Boone stood silently, scanning the area, both of them solemn and focused.

"He liked cryptology. It was his thing when he was a teen."

"We'll look for a coded message, then," Cyrus responded, his gaze shifting back to her. She felt the weight of his stare, the intensity. He had the darkest eyes she'd ever seen. Nearly black, the pupils and irises blending into each other. "Just so you know, you're going to have to start following the rules. It's going to be way too difficult to keep you alive if you don't."

"Do you really think Elijah would risk trying to kill me? The sheriff is already suspicious. If something happened to me, he'd be even more so."

"He can be as suspicious as he wants. Without evidence of a crime, there isn't a whole lot he can do. I think your husband's death proves that more than just about anything else could. You said yourself that one of Joshua's friends disappeared. How difficult would it be for them to make the same thing happen to you?"

Not very, she would have answered if Stella hadn't pulled up in a black SUV. She hopped out, opened the back door, nearly shoved Lark inside. "Head for the center. Cyrus and Chance—"

"And Boone," Chance interrupted, walking

to the front passenger seat and climbing in, the box Elijah had brought in his hands.

Stella scowled, but didn't argue. "Suit yourself, *boss*."

There was an emphasis on the last word that Lark didn't miss.

Not her business, but she *was* curious.

Cyrus climbed in beside her, closed the door, grabbed his seat belt, his fingers brushing her hip. Warmth shot through her, and she blushed, her cheeks so hot, she wanted to press her palms to them.

She looked away, realized that Boone was climbing in the SUV, folding his long legs, a half smile on his face. He'd noticed. She was sure of it.

He didn't say a word, just buckled his seat belt and tapped Stella on the shoulder. "Let's go. I'm hungry."

Stella muttered something under her breath but pulled out of the parking lot, the trees whizzing by as she picked up speed and merged onto the highway.

ELEVEN

They made it to Baltimore in record time, the traffic light, the trip uneventful. It had been three months since Lark had been in her neighborhood, but it felt like she'd never left. The quaint brownstone still had a red door. The exterior staircase leading to her second-floor apartment was still a little rusted. She had one neighbor above. One below. One to the left of the apartment who she'd only met a couple of times. To the right, an alley separated her building from another. Twenty years ago, the rows of brownstones had been neglected and mostly abandoned. Now the entire block had been returned to its former glory.

Stella found street parking in front of the building, and Chance jumped out of the SUV, jogging up the stairs ahead of everyone, jiggling the doorknob. "Locked," he called.

"The key is in the box." Lark unbuckled her belt, leaned over the seat, digging through the box until she had the keys, her wallet, her cell phone. It felt odd to be holding them again. Like she'd been sleepwalking and suddenly woken unsure of where she was or how she'd gotten there.

"He was making sure no one unlocked the door before we got here," Cyrus said as he got out, offered his hand and pulled Lark to her feet. He towered over her. Nearly a foot taller, but he didn't make her feel small or weak. As a matter of fact, she felt stronger when he was around, more capable. It was the way she'd felt with Joshua, and remembering that made her stomach churn.

"You don't think Elijah sent someone here, do you?" she asked, eying the metal stairs, the landing, the little welcome mat in front of the door.

"It's not about what I think," Cyrus replied. "What matters is being prepared for whatever might happen."

She didn't like the sound of that.

She didn't particularly like thinking about all the things that could happen or might happen. She'd always been a planner, had always enjoyed creating order out of chaos. Her childhood had taught her the value of working hard. Her mother had set an example of everything Lark hadn't wanted to be.

Not that she hadn't loved Katie. She had. She just hadn't been able to depend on her. She hadn't been able to count on coming home to a clean house, a home-cooked meal, a parent who asked if she had homework. She hadn't been able to count on the electricity being on or food being in the refrigerator. By the time she was nine, she was helping elderly neighbors with yard work to earn money for school clothes. Right around the time she turned twelve, she'd started using whatever money she had to pay whatever bills that she could.

As a kid, she'd spent too many hours worrying about things that no kid should ever worry about. As an adult, she'd tried hard to break the cycle of worry, tried to let go of her need to control. God knew. He provided. And Lark was careful about her money, her bills, her choices. She had a little nest egg in savings, plenty of money in her checking account. She didn't need or want big or fancy. All she wanted was security.

She'd had it for a while.

Then it had been taken from her.

For months after Joshua's death, she'd felt the heavy weight of anxiety. It had lain on her chest, cut off her breath, made thinking about anything but her worries nearly impossible. Living in a car, trying to find a job, mourning Joshua's loss. Those things had turned her into a basket case of nervous energy and angst.

She wasn't going there again. She wasn't going to dwell on the possibilities, wasn't going to carry anxiety and stress. Whatever was going to happen, God was in control. He knew the plan for Lark's life, and she trusted that it was a good one.

That was enough to get her moving up the steps.

Her feet clanged on the metal, her hand gliding over the handrail. It was cool and a little rough beneath her hands.

Cyrus crowded in behind her. Chance waited ahead, his gaze focused on the alley below.

Did he expect someone to be there?

One of Elijah's men, maybe?

It wasn't like the apartment's location was a secret. She'd stayed in contact with Eric and Maria during the time she'd been away from the compound. She'd sent them her address and phone number, emailed them a few times. They'd only responded once. The invitation to visit Amos Way had come as a surprise.

In light of everything that had happened, it made sense.

Elijah had probably planted a seed in Eric's head, made him think that having Lark back would help with the grieving process.

She reached the landing, skirted past Chance, had the keys in the lock, when Cyrus touched her shoulder.

"Let me," he said, his thumb brushing her neck, that one touch sending heat shooting through her.

She dropped her hand from the knob, tried to move out of the way, but Cyrus was behind her, Boone to one side, Chance to the other. There was nowhere to go, and she stood stiffly as Cyrus reached around, turned the key in the lock.

If he sensed her tension, he didn't mention it. Just cupped both her shoulders, moved her toward Boone.

"I'll take a look."

"I'll—" *Come*, she was going to say, but he'd already stepped into the small foyer, his broad shoulders blocking her view of the living room and kitchen beyond.

He paused, motioned something with his left hand.

The next thing Lark knew, she was being hurried back down the steps, rushed into the SUV. Chance stood beside her window, his coat opened to reveal a gun holster strapped to his chest, his crisp white shirt and dress slacks making him look like a secret service agent or a bodyguard.

She tapped on the glass.

He ignored her.

She scooted across the seat, realized that Boone was already there, blocking her view of the street. She wasn't sure where Stella had gone.

Into the apartment with Cyrus?

Had he seen something? Heard something?

She pulled her cell phone from her pocket, turned it on. Still fully charged. Essex had texted a few dozen times, and she read through each message, could almost feel him growing more frantic. She'd texted him quickly, let him know that she was alive and at home.

Almost at home.

She frowned, tapped on the glass again.

Like his boss, Boone refused to turn around.

She scrambled into the front seat, eyed her still-open front door. No sign of Cyrus or Stella. She reached for the door handle, stopped when Chance appeared.

He yanked the door open, bent so that they were eye to eye. He had the bluest eyes she'd ever seen, the hardest expression. Not a nice guy. A driven one. "That," he ground out, "is not a good idea."

"Why?"

"Someone has been in your apartment. Cyrus and Stella are doing a walk-through.

Once they're finished, we'll bring you up. Now, get into the backseat. It'll be a little more difficult for a bullet to reach you there."

"What about you and Boone?"

"No one is gunning for us, Lark. You're the one Elijah wants dead."

True. And that was enough to get her moving. She climbed into the back, slouched in the seat as if doing so could keep a bullet from hitting her. She'd seen what one could do. Sheriff Johnson had impounded her Mustang and planned to send it to the state police for forensic testing, but the entire back window had been shattered, the front window cracked.

Minutes ticked by. They felt like hours.

The sun beat down on the SUV upping the temperature in the vehicle. She felt like she was baking alive, but didn't bother knocking on the glass again. She just stripped out of Boone's coat, set it on the seat back and waited.

Finally, Chance opened the door, gestured for her to exit the car. He was all business as he took her arm, hurried her up the steps. No words either. No explanation of what had been found.

She stepped into the foyer, stopped short. She'd left the place orderly and neat. Now it was chaos—couch cushions tossed on the floor, flour spilled out onto the counters, cupboards open, broken plates spread across the kitchen.

"What in the world!" she breathed, taking a step deeper into the house.

Cyrus stood in the living room, snapping pictures with his cell phone. He looked up as she approached, a smile easing the hard lines of his face. "Your cheeks are pink."

"The SUV was getting hot."

"Sorry it took so long. We wanted to make sure it was safe. The good news is…" He snapped a picture of her favorite Goodwill lamp. It lay on its side, the depression era glass shattered. "The apartment is empty."

"The bad news is, it's been destroyed," she responded.

He stopped taking pictures, focused his attention on Lark. "You're right. It has been. That's a tough thing, Lark, to see all this lying around broken. But you're strong enough to deal with it."

"How do you know how strong I am?" she responded, picking up a book and setting it on the now-empty shelf.

"I've seen you in action, remember?" he said, snapping a couple more pictures. "If there's anything missing, you'll have to make an itemized list for the police."

"The television is still here. My desktop."

She touched the computer monitor that still sat on the antique desk the owner had left in the apartment. It had been there for decades, and he'd wanted it to stay. She'd been careful with it, covering the top with a sheet of Plexiglas to protect the wood.

The intruder hadn't been interested in the desk or the computer. He'd emptied all the drawers, though, scattering papers and checkbooks across the room.

"He left your checkbooks, too," Cyrus pointed out. "Your bank records."

"I guess the desk wasn't the best place to keep that stuff." She lifted a small box that she'd stored in the bottom drawer of the desk. She kept cash there for emergencies. It was empty, the lid torn from the hinges. "I had a hundred dollars in here. It's—"

"Here," Stella called from the kitchen. "Sitting on top of a pile of flour and sugar that's been dumped."

So…not a robbery. That much was clear.

In Lark's mind, that only left one option. Elijah had visited her apartment or sent someone else to do it.

"I wonder if they found what they were looking for?" she murmured as she walked down the hall.

"Joshua's things?" Cyrus asked.

"I can't imagine they were looking for anything else. I don't have a lot of valuables, but the money was there, my bank statement, my checks. They could have robbed me blind, if they'd wanted to."

She walked into her bedroom, stopping just past the threshold. She'd always loved the room, the three large windows that bathed it with sunlight, the high tray ceiling, the built-in wardrobe in the corner. She'd hung her wedding photo on the wall, put up the little wooden plaque that Joshua had made her for their first anniversary.

Both lay on the floor, the plaque half covered by one of her shirts. The mattress had been tossed from the bed, linens lying in a heap beside it. Her pillow had been slashed, the stuffing pulled out.

"They were thorough," she said, stepping over an empty dresser drawer.

"Where were you keeping Joshua's things?" Cyrus asked, crouching near their wedding photo, carefully lifting the picture from the broken glass and busted frame.

"In the closet," she said, turning away because she didn't want to see Joshua's smiling face, didn't want to think about how happy and positive he'd been when they'd met.

She'd loved that about him. The way he

always looked for the positive, the grace he extended to the people around him, to the world in general. She'd never heard him speak a bad word about anyone. Not until Ethan's disappearance. Even then, he'd said little.

She walked into the closet, flicking on the light. The building owner had converted a small bedroom into a walk-in. Lark hadn't had much to store in it. Her work clothes. A few workout outfits. She'd bought a vintage desk, shoved it against one wall, put a laptop on it. Sometimes, when the apartment seemed too big for one person, when its silence pressed in and made her long to go back in time, recapture the joy of having someone to share life with, she'd grade papers in there, her earbuds in, doing everything she could to forget that she'd ever had anything different.

The chair she used had been tipped over. She set it upright, climbed onto it. There were cupboards at the top of the closet. Too high for her to reach, so she'd never used them. She had looked in them when she'd moved in, checking to make sure they were empty, that the previous renter hadn't left anything behind. She'd found the back panel of one of the cupboards lying on its side. Behind it, the wall was open, revealing pipes that the owner must have wanted easy access to. There wasn't a lot of space, but it was enough for her to hide the things that meant the most to her.

She yanked open the cupboard, standing on her toes and peering into the darkness. The panel was still in place, and she nearly tipped the chair in her hurry to remove it.

"Careful." Cyrus grabbed her waist, held her steady as she leaned in. She could feel the imprint of his fingers through her T-shirt, and her pulse raced.

Fear. Adrenaline. Those were the excuses she wanted to make, but she'd always tried to be honest with herself and everyone else. She knew physical attraction when she felt it, had ignored it plenty of times in the past. After all, a good relationship was built on a lot more.

The problem was, Cyrus was likeable. All his toughness, all his gruffness, all his determination and focus, she admired them. She liked that he didn't pity her, that he pushed her to be her best self, to keep being strong rather letting other people be strong for her. He didn't need to be her protector, and he knew it, but he wanted to be there for her. That meant more than a handsome face, a sweet word, a stunning smile. To Lark, it was everything.

"See anything?" he asked, and she forced herself to focus, to concentrate on getting the box, making sure that everything was exactly where she'd left it.

She pried the panel away, reached into the wall behind it.

The box was there, the metal cool beneath her fingers.

She dragged it out, jumped down from the chair, brushed a layer of dust from the top of the box. "It's here!"

"Is everything still in it?" Cyrus leaned in close, his chest pressed against her back, his fingers cupping her elbow.

"I hope so," she responded, her fingers shaking as she fiddled with the lock, tried to get the correct combination.

"Come on," she muttered, and Cyrus took the box from her hand, used a tiny pick to open the lock.

The lid popped open.

She saw the shirt first, the soft blue flannel, making her heart ache and her vision blur. She lifted it, pressing it to her nose. Not a hint of Joshua remained.

"I wish that I could bring him back for you," Cyrus said quietly, turning her around, pulling her into his arms, the shirt smashed between them, the box he still held bumping against her shoulder.

The words—so simple, so sincere—speared

her heart, because she knew they were true. She knew that if he'd had the ability, Cyrus would have risked everything to bring Joshua home to her.

"Thank you," she said, wrapping her arms around his waist, burying her head in the crisp white cotton of his shirt. She could feel the slow thud of his heart, the gentle rise and fall of his breath, and she thought that if she stayed there long enough, the ache of losing Joshua would hurt just a little bit less.

"Okay?" he asked, cupping her jaw, looking into her eyes.

He had a way of doing that, of focusing on her so completely that it seemed she was all that existed, all that mattered.

She nodded, swallowing down the roughest edges of sorrow, taking the box from his hand. The Bible was there, the leather cover soft and worn, the edges of the pages curled and folded from years of being turned.

Beneath that, Joshua's wedding ring lay glinting in the overhead light. She lifted it, slid it onto her thumb. "He never got to wear it. Elijah thought jewelry was a sign of arrogance and pride. I bought it for Joshua anyway, because I wanted there to be some symbol of what we shared."

"Did he give you one?"

"Yes." She smiled, remembering how surprised she'd been by the gift. "I sewed it into the hem of one of my skirts. Every time I wore that skirt, I smiled a little more brightly."

"Do you still have the ring?" he asked, glancing at her hand.

"No. I had to turn in all my skirts and sweaters when I left the compound. I wasn't thinking clearly, or I would have cut the ring out before I left. I tried to find it when I went back, but I think they gave the skirt to someone else. She probably doesn't even know she's wearing my wedding ring."

"Maybe you'll get it back one day." He put the Bible back in the box. "And you can wear it on your finger, so the world can see it, and know you were married to a great man."

"That's really sweet, Cyrus," she said, and he frowned.

"Another thing that I would prefer you not mention to anyone at HEART."

She smiled, and he chucked her under the chin, took her hand. "The police should be here soon. Let's wait for them in the foyer. Once they're done, we'll clean things up and get out of here."

"Where are we going to go?"

"HEART has a couple of properties. The one we're going to—"

The middle window exploded, glass shattering, fire shooting up the curtains, licking at the ceiling.

Smoke filled the room, turning light to dark so quickly that Lark stumbled, her hand slipping from Cyrus's. She thought he was gone, rushing through the darkness ahead of her, and she dropped to her knees, Joshua's shirt still clutched in her hand, heat blasting her face.

She coughed, inhaling more of the noxious fumes as she tried to clear her lungs.

She had to get out, had to escape.

Someone grabbed her waist, hauled her up and out of the room.

They'd been set up. Knowing that made Cyrus furious.

He carried Lark through the hall, fighting the need to inhale more deeply, to gasp for more air. There was none to be had. The apartment was filled with smoke, flames already crawling along Lark's bedroom door.

He was blinded by the heat, confused by the smoke.

One way led to a dead end. The other to the living room.

If he chose wrong, he might not have a chance to choose again.

"This way!" Stella yelled, suddenly in front of him, her figure just a shadow through the smoke.

She grabbed his sore arm, dragged him through the hallway.

He trusted her implicitly, went with her because she'd proven herself invaluable time and time again.

They made it to the living room, heat building, the air seeming to undulate with it.

Boone and Chance were at the door, and they flanked him as he exited the building, stuck close as he ran down the stairs.

Stella was in the SUV before he reached it, engine running, gun drawn. She eyed the building across the alley from Lark's.

"It came from that building. The window on the second floor is open. It wasn't before."

"Rocket launcher," Chance said. "Nothing else could have done that kind of damage. Boone, ride with Stella. We'll keep you posted."

Cyrus set Lark in the seat, looked into her face. Soot smudged her cheeks, coated her hair. "Stella and Boone will take you to the safe house."

"What about—?"

He dropped the lockbox in her lap, shut the door, slapped the hood.

He didn't have time to explain how things were going to work.

Someone had lain in wait for them. Someone who'd known they were heading back to Maryland. Someone who had a lot to gain by destroying evidence and silencing Lark.

He didn't wait for Chance to come up with a plan. Just took the Glock his boss offered and ran toward the alley.

TWELVE

"You get yourself killed," Chance growled, racing along beside him, "and I'm not going to be happy."

"Don't feel like hunting up another team member?" he asked, eyeing the fire escape beneath the open window. It hadn't been lowered. The guy must have found another way in.

"Don't feel like losing another friend," Chance responded. "But I think the guy is gone. If he isn't, he's a fool."

"He's a fool either way." Cyrus tucked the Glock into his waistband, grabbed the edge of the fire escape and pulled himself up. Sirens screamed as a police car sped into the alley, squealed to a stop just below.

Chance could deal with the officer who got out of the car. Cyrus had other things on his mind.

He kept low, moving toward the open window, waiting for several heartbeats, the Glock in his hand. Familiar. Comforting. Blood seeped from the wound in his arm. He'd popped some stitches, but he'd deal with that later.

The officer shouted something, but Cyrus wasn't in the mood for listening. If Lark had been anywhere near the window of her bedroom, she'd be dead.

Nothing moved in the window opening, and he peered in cautious. Ready.

No furniture in the room. No rug on the floor. Something was there, though, and he recognized it immediately. An RPG-7. Not something he'd ever seen used in the United States, but he'd seen it plenty when he'd served in Iraq.

He didn't touch it, just moved past, staying close to the wall as he eased out into a wide hallway. The place felt empty, but he didn't take any chances, moving through each room cautiously, the acrid scent of smoke tingeing the air.

The apartment was larger than Lark's. Three bedrooms. A bathroom. The old wood floor scuffed and covered in dust. He crouched, eyeing a boot print pressed in the middle of the living room floor. He snapped a photo, found another print near the apartment door.

Someone had tampered with the lock, and the door was cracked open, sunlight filtering in. He opened it, scowling as he realized he was standing on a landing above a busy street. Nowhere for the perp to go but down. He'd probably had a car waiting, was probably a couple of miles away by now.

A female police officer sprinted toward him, taking the stairs two at a time. "Sir! Drop your weapon! Put your hands up!"

Cyrus didn't try to explain who he was or what he was doing. He did what he was told, lowering the gun without raising the barrel, setting it on the ground.

He had his hands up before he straightened, allowed himself to be cuffed and patted down. There was no sense trying to reason with someone in a situation like this. Tensions were too high.

"Cyrus Mitchell?" the officer said, his wallet open in her hand, his ID clearly visible.

"That's right."

"You have a reason for being in this apartment?"

"Someone fired a rocket launcher into the building next door. I'm sure you noticed the smoke," he responded, not quite able to hold back his sarcasm.

It didn't earn him any brownie points.

The officer frowned, closing the wallet, and calling something into her radio.

"While we're standing here, the guy who

fired the launcher is getting farther away," he offered, and her frown deepened.

"Sir, for all I know, you're the one who fired it."

"If I had, I wouldn't have stuck around and waited for you to arrive."

"I've seen stranger things," she muttered, taking his arm. "How about you show me where this rocket launcher is?"

Cyrus complied, because he didn't have much of a choice, and because he wanted to get a better look at the RPG-7. It had to have been smuggled into the United States. Probably carried across the border from Mexico and trucked up through the center of the country. And probably not brought in alone.

Was it possible that's what the boxes delivered to Amos Way had contained?

The thought made his blood run cold.

If he hadn't been cuffed, he'd have called Chance, asked him to get up there stat. If Elijah was smuggling in arms like the rocket launcher, he was planning something bigger than just making money. This kind of smuggling required deep pockets and deeper connections.

The officer snapped a couple of pictures of the launcher, peered out the window and snapped a photo from there. He wanted to tell her that the clock was ticking, that they needed to get the DEA involved, question the neighbors.

He doubted she'd appreciate his input, so he kept quiet, standing right where she'd left him, smoke from the fire at Lark's place filling his lungs and stinging his nose.

"Cyrus!" Chance called, his voice echoing through the empty apartment.

"Back here," Cyrus responded. "Cuffed and ready for transportation."

The officer turned, eyeing Chance as he walked into the room, two police officers right behind him.

Thirty seconds later, Cyrus was free, rubbing his wrists and crouching next to the launcher.

"Russian," Chance said, and he nodded.

"Can't say I've ever seen one before," one of the officers cut in. "And I don't like that I'm seeing one now."

"I'm calling in the DEA. We'll see what they have to say." The female officer shot the words over her shoulder as she walked out of the room.

Cyrus knew she was probably thinking the same thing as he was. If there was one rocket launcher in civilian hands, there were probably more of them. With a weapon like this one, any hands were the wrong ones. It was a weapon of war.

Apparently, right now, someone was at war against Lark.

He pulled out his cell phone.

He needed to be where he was, but he also needed to be sure Lark was okay.

Lark was supposed to be sleeping.

She was pacing instead, the floorboards of the old farmhouse creaking under her feet. Boone and Stella had brought her there nearly ten hours ago. They'd given her clothes, shampoo, soap. They'd escorted her to the third floor, led her into what had once been an attic. Now it was a large bedroom with an attached bathroom and thickly curtained windows. Stella had gone over the rules. The gist of them was that Lark was to stay in the house, stay away from the windows, resist the urge to text or call people she knew.

That had been difficult.

Essex had called three times, texted ten. He'd seen the news, knew her apartment had been destroyed. He was worried.

She was, too.

She'd known Elijah was using Amos Way as a front for something, but she'd never imagined it was something so big that he'd chase her across state lines to stop her from revealing it.

She'd imagined him trafficking in drugs,

maybe selling illegal firearms. It was something more than that. She knew it. She just didn't know what.

She'd had a long time to think about it, a lot of hours when she'd sat in the kitchen of the old house or in the living room, twiddling her thumbs and hoping that Cyrus or Chance would call.

If either had, she hadn't heard about it.

Boone had assured her that they were fine, that he and Stella would have been contacted if either was injured.

She guessed they knew the way HEART worked better than she did, but she was still concerned.

When Stella had suggested she get some rest, she'd agreed. Mostly because she didn't know what else to do.

She'd been in the room ever since, waiting, worrying, waiting, praying. Probably she should be praying more and worrying less. That's what Joshua would have said.

He'd have been right, but she couldn't stop the thoughts that were running through her head. She couldn't seem to just give it over to God and trust that He had it all under control.

She'd tried to distract herself. She'd taken a shower, scrubbed her skin until it hurt, the flowery soap she'd found near the sink masking the horrible stench of smoke that had clung to her for the entire three-hour drive. She was sure she smelled it again, barely hidden by the soap and the fruity shampoo. She'd used half a bottle of that. Brushed her hair, braided it, put on soft flannel pajamas that Stella had given her. The clothes she'd had on had been tossed in a plastic bag and handed to Stella, who always seemed to be just outside the door when Lark opened it.

A personal bodyguard? It seemed that way.

Lark couldn't imagine that she'd need one. Not where she was. The house was so far off the beaten path, she doubted anyone could find it. When she'd asked, Boone had said they were in western Maryland, right outside the small town of River Valley. Only one road led to the house, and that dead-ended in a heavily forested area that could only be accessed by foot.

She'd be safe there, she'd been assured.

She didn't feel safe.

She felt scared.

She sat on the bed, grabbed the lockbox she'd put there. She'd been surprised that Cyrus had carried it from the house. He could have dropped it. Maybe he even should have, but he'd held on to it, made sure that she'd had it before he'd left.

She opened it, pulled out the flannel shirt

that Stella had run through the wash five times. It didn't smell like smoke anymore. It smelled like fabric softener and detergent.

She shoved her arms through the sleeves like she'd done dozens of times when Joshua was alive, wishing that she was wrapping herself in his arms instead. His wedding ring glinted on her thumb as she took the Bible from the box.

It was the one thing he'd valued more than anything else. More than the rifle he'd inherited from his grandfather. More than the beautiful carvings he'd created. More than his tools, his shop behind his parents' house.

A tear dropped onto the faded cover, and she wiped it away.

Joshua wouldn't have wanted her to grieve forever. He wouldn't have wanted her to grieve at all. To him, death was simply a change in status and form, a new venue for the soul.

Another tear dripped onto the Bible, and she stood, impatient with herself. She hadn't cried in months, hated tears almost as much as she hated being holed up in a house while other people fought her battles. And that's what this was. A battle for the truth, and she was going to find it.

She carried the Bible across the room, stood in front of heavily curtained windows. She knew what she'd been told, she knew what she wasn't supposed to do.

Right at that moment, she didn't really care. She flicked off the lamp, plunged the room into darkness and pulled back the curtains.

The moon hung low in the sky, bathing distant treetops in gold and illuminating a large empty expanse of grass. The backyard. That's what she was looking at. No trees. No shrubs. Nothing for anyone to hide behind. She knew that was planned. Just like the dead-end road and the lack of neighbors was planned.

She unlocked the window, cracked it open, let early fall air sweep in. Nothing changed. No alarm sounded. No one pounded up the stairs and banged on her door. She wanted to be outside, sitting on the porch swing that hung from the eves, listening to the quiet sounds of rural life.

She grabbed her phone from the dresser. Essex had left another message. He'd spoken with Cyrus, was glad that she was okay.

She was glad one of them had spoken to Cyrus.

Not that she was bitter about it or anything, but it would have been nice to hear his voice, to know for sure that he was okay. He didn't have her phone number, but he could have called Stella or Boone, asked to speak to Lark. Better yet, he could have showed up at the farmhouse, filled her in on what they'd found, let her see for herself that he'd survived.

She frowned, surprised by how much she wanted to hear his voice, to see his face.

She paced back to the window, settled into the rocking chair there, Joshua's Bible in her lap, his shirt warming her.

She missed him every day. She always would, but maybe there was room in her life for something more than a lonely apartment, a job, her volunteer work.

She fingered the edges of the Bible, praying for the comfort she knew would come, the peace that she knew she would find. Eventually. For now, she let the cool breeze and the soft country sounds fill her mind.

She must have drifted off, because the creak of floorboards outside the room jerked her awake. She jumped up, the Bible clutched to her chest, the remnants of a nightmare still clinging to her mind.

The board creaked again, and her pulse jumped.

Someone was out there. Stella? Boone? Maybe they'd heard from Cyrus.

She flicked on the light, hurried to the door, yanked it open.

Cyrus stood in the hall, white shirt still covered with soot, eyes shadowed from too many hours of work and not enough sleep. Somehow, he still looked good.

"Did I wake you?" he asked, walking into the room, carrying the scent of smoke with him.

"Not really."

"Which means I did." He smiled. "I should have waited until morning."

"If you had, I'd have woken in an hour, worrying and wondering what was going on." She gestured to the rocking chair. "You should sit down. You look exhausted."

"*You* should follow the rules," he replied, crossing the room, shutting the window and pulling the curtains closed. "And I'm not going to sit down, because I'm still covered with soot, and Stella won't be happy if I smudge the fabric on that rocker."

"We can go downstairs. The kitchen chairs are wood."

"And the coffeepot is full, but," he added, "I'm filled to the brim with coffee, and we're both tired, so it's probably better if I say what I have to say and let you get back to sleep."

Say what had he to say?

That didn't sound good. Lark pulled the Bible a little closer, braced herself for whatever he was going to say. "What's going on?"

"We found a rocket launcher in the apartment across the alley from yours. The DEA is investigating, trying to figure out how it got into the country and into civilian hands. I suggested they take a look at Amos Way, search the storage sheds there."

"Did they?"

"They planned to, but they were on their way there when they got word that a fire had swept through the compound. It destroyed half the buildings."

"What!" She'd been anticipating a lot of things, but not that. "Are they sure?"

"The DEA usually is. Sheriff Johnson called me an hour later. He said that all four storage sheds were destroyed. If there were any firearms or weapons there, they were removed before the fire. Whatever evidence was left was burned to ashes."

"Convenient," she said absently, her thoughts on the people she'd grown to care about. Men and women who really did believe that Amos Way was a sanctuary from the world.

Her in-laws. Their other children. Joshua's nieces and nephews. Friends who had taught her how to quilt, sew, cook.

"That's what the sheriff thinks. What we all think."

"Was anyone hurt?"

"Your father-in-law is in the hospital. He was burned while trying to put out the fire."

"Is he okay?"

"I'm not sure. Several people were injured. When I spoke with the sheriff, he didn't have any information on their conditions."

"I need to go see him," she said, grabbing her phone and her purse and heading for the door.

He snagged the back of Joshua's shirt, pulled her to a stop. "Let's not go off half-cocked, Lark."

"I'm going to the hospital to visit my father-in-law. I don't think that can be classified as half-cocked."

"And yet, you're about to head outside in flannel pajamas with bare feet."

He had a point, and she hurried to the closet, took her sturdy Amos Way shoes from it, slipped them on.

"Better?" she asked, turning to face Cyrus again.

He'd moved closer, and she could see flecks of gold in his brown eyes, see the tiny lines at the corner of his mouth. "Only if you plan to sleep in them."

"I think we're at cross purposes, Cyrus," she muttered, refusing to back down. Despite everything that had happened, despite everything she knew to be true about Amos Way, she had to go back to Pennsylvania.

"Not if your purpose is to stay alive, because my purpose is to keep you that way."

"My purpose is to get back to Pennsylvania so that—"

"You can be with your father-in-law. Yeah. I know, but being with him isn't going to change his prognosis, and it isn't going to make things any easier on him. It's only going to make them easier on you."

"I'm not going there to make things easier on myself," she replied, her cheeks hot. "I'm going to make them easier on Maria. She's not good at handling stress, and she's not going to know how to navigate the medical system. She's spent most of the past thirty years in that compound."

"There will be people there who can help her."

"She needs me there."

"Why?" he asked, the word hard and cold, his face expressionless. He didn't look like the guy who'd sat on the steps next to her, the one who'd made her feel like she wasn't alone. He looked like one of John's thugs, and she took a step away, raised her chin a notch.

"Because, I'm family."

"She has other family."

It was true. She had other children. She had a community that would rally around her.

"The thing is, Lark," he said, his voice gentling, his fingers light as he brushed a strand of hair from her cheek, straightened the collar of Joshua's shirt. "You're letting your emotions force you into a decision. You're thinking with your heart instead of your head. That would be great, if Elijah wasn't gunning for you. But I think what happened at your apartment proves that he is. Give me and the team a couple of days to work some things out. Then, I'll bring you back to Pennsylvania, okay?"

Three seconds ago, she would have said it wasn't, but she couldn't resist Cyrus's gentleness any more than she could deny the validity of his words. Rushing back to Pennsylvania could get her killed. It could also get Cyrus or one of his team members killed.

"Okay."

"Good." He smiled, and her heart jumped in response, her fingers itching to touch the rough stubble on his chin, to brush soot from his cheek.

"You need to get some rest," she said instead.

"So do you. First, though, I have something for you." He reached in his pocket, pulled out a folded piece of paper. "It's just a copy of the envelope the note was in. I thought you might like to have it. The original has been sent to the state police. Their handwriting expert is comparing the writing on the envelope and on the note."

She took the paper from his hand, looked at the curled *L* and the heart-shaped *A*, thought about how Joshua had bent over the paper, scrawled her name.

"Don't let it make you sad, Lark," Cyrus said. "Let it make you grateful that you had the kind of love you did. Even if it was for a shorter time than you wanted."

He was out the door and down the stairs before she could respond. Before she could do what she wanted and ask if he'd ever had someone he loved deeply, who he missed avidly.

She folded the paper, tucked it into the Bible, sat back in the rocker and waited for morning to come.

THIRTEEN

Five days.

That's how long Lark had been cooped up in the farmhouse.

She'd followed the rules.

She hadn't complained about not seeing her in-laws, hadn't begged to be allowed to leave. Cyrus had been correct when he'd said they had common goals, and she was trying hard to be part of the team.

She was getting antsy, though.

She asked for updates a couple of times a day. Cyrus always gave them, but there wasn't a whole lot of information. They did know that the writing on the envelope didn't match the writing in the letter, that the blood was Joshua's, that it was likely it had been at the scene and splatted by his blood when he was shot.

Lark didn't like thinking about that, but she hadn't been able to stop. Not since Cyrus had given her the information. The police were opening an investigation, but nearly two years after Joshua's death, they weren't sure how much evidence they'd be able to collect.

She paced her bedroom, glanced at her watch. Stella had said they'd be eating at seven. Lark didn't plan to go down to the kitchen. She wasn't hungry. Hadn't really been hungry since she'd arrived. She fingered the scab on her wrist. Her bruises had faded, the wound on her wrist was almost completely healed, and she wasn't any closer to proving that Elijah was responsible for Joshua's death.

Maybe that wasn't her place.

Maybe seeking justice wasn't her right.

She'd been thinking about that at night when she couldn't sleep, thinking about how God's will was going to be done, regardless of her work or lack of it.

She still hated being prisoner in the safe house.

She wanted fresh air, sunshine, a nice long jog in the cool fall air.

She dropped into the rocking chair, took Joshua's Bible from the table beside it and opened it. There were notes in nearly every margin, highlighted passages on nearly every page. She'd been reading some of his notes, the past few days, studying passages. A few pages had been clearly earmarked, key passages highlighted in blue or green or pink rather than the yellow highlighter Joshua had always used.

Seeing those passages made her smile. Joshua had always had a love for learning and a vivid imagination. For all she knew, he'd color-coded sections according to subject. Maybe he'd used different colors depending on how much he'd enjoyed the passage or how meaningful it was to him.

Someone tapped on the door.

Not Stella's quick rap. Not Boone's loud knock.

Cyrus.

She knew the way he tapped his fingertips against the wood, just barely making noise because he never wanted to wake her if she was sleeping.

She stood, ran her hand over her hair, smoothing the strands as she called for him to come in.

The door opened, and he filled the threshold, his dark gaze dropping from her face to the front of her shirt, his lips quirking.

"What?" she said, knowing exactly what he was looking at.

"Pink is a good color on you."

"Even when it's pink poodles on purple cotton?" she asked, and he laughed.

"Even then."

"It was in one of the drawers. Stella said I could use whatever I found."

"And you chose that, huh?"

"It made me smile. I kind of needed that today."

"And I needed a laugh, so thanks." He sat on the edge of the bed, his long legs encased in faded denim, his dark T-shirt clinging to a muscular chest. It was his eyes that always caught her attention, though, the depth of them, the deep blackness of the irises. "Stella made dinner."

"She told me she was going to."

"You're not going to eat?"

"I'm not hungry."

"Still worrying about your father-in-law?"

"Among other things."

"I heard from Sheriff Johnson. He said Eric's condition has been upgraded from critical to stable. He's able to have visitors. If you want to go, I'll take you."

"Now?"

"Chance thinks that's the best option. A midnight visit to the hospital probably isn't something Elijah will be expecting."

"You don't agree?" she asked as she shoved her feet into tennis shoes she'd found in the closet, grabbed a black cardigan from the hanger.

"I don't want you anywhere near Amos Way or River Fork, Lark. I think you know that."

"But you're offering to take me," she pointed out.

"You want to go. Chance wants you to go. Sheriff Johnson wants you to go. And I'm pretty confident Elijah Clayton is counting on you showing up."

"I understand why Elijah wants me there, but I'm not so sure why Chance and Sheriff Johnson would care."

"They think your presence might force Elijah to make a move."

"So I'm the bait in their trap."

"That's one way of looking at it."

"Is there another?"

"You're a pawn in a very deadly game, and you're being used." He bit the words out.

"I can only be used if I allow myself to be."

"And you're going to." He stood, stalked to the door. "I'm against this. I want to make that clear."

"Okay." She shrugged into the cardigan, shoved her cell phone in her pocket.

"That's it?" he demanded.

"I don't know what else to say."

"Maybe that you'd rather stay here. Where it's safe. That you'd rather let Sheriff Johnson and the state police figure things out."

"I wouldn't," she responded, lifting Joshua's Bible, feeling the worn leather beneath her palm. "Joshua deserves justice, and I've been thinking that maybe I deserve the opportunity to move on."

His expression softened, and he took the Bible from her hands. "He read this a lot."

"He studied it a lot. Look inside. Every other passage is highlighted."

He opened it, turned a few pages. "Odd."

"What?" She leaned in close, felt the warmth of his arm, the thick pad of the bandage that still covered his biceps.

"Random words highlighted. A couple sets of them. A few numbers circled and others squared. Did you notice?"

"I noticed that he used different colors, but I guess I didn't pay much attention to how many words were in a highlighted section."

Cyrus nodded, a deep frown line etched in his forehead. "Mind if we take this along? I'd like to take a closer look."

"I was planning to bring it. I've been reading it every night."

"It makes you feel closer to Joshua?" He cupped her elbow, led her out into the hall.

"It makes me feel closer to God. I need that right now. I need to feel like He's in control, because I know I'm not."

"Funny. I was thinking the same thing a few minutes ago."

"That God is in control?"

"That I'm not." He started down the steps, his fingers still warm on her arm. "So, I guess He's what we've got."

"That's plenty, Cyrus. You know that right?"

"I'm learning it." He smiled, shrugged. "It's hard for someone like me. We like to think we've got it all figured out, that if we push hard enough and work hard enough, life will be what we want. Eventually, we figure it out, though. Eventually, we understand that there are better plans then our own. That God's will is always worked out. Exactly the way He wants."

"I'm sorry you don't want me to do this, Cyrus," she said, because she was suddenly very sorry that she couldn't give him what he wanted, stay in the safe house hiding away until someone else brought Elijah down.

"I understand why you have to."

They reached the foyer, and he touched her cheek. "Just follow the rules, okay? Do what we tell you? Don't try to be a hero, because it could get you killed. That won't be okay with me, Lark. Not by a long shot." He kissed her forehead, his lips just grazing her skin.

She felt it to her core, felt her world rock and then right itself, felt everything that she'd thought she'd never have again suddenly there, right within her reach.

"Ready?" Chance called, his footsteps tapping on the wood floor.

Cyrus stepped away, but the feeling lingered as Chance strode toward them and opened the front door.

Chance's question had been rhetorical, but Cyrus was tempted to answer.

He *wasn't* ready, because he didn't want to bring Lark back to River Fork. He and Chance had already had it out. They'd gone back and forth on the plan, debating the merits of Lark returning to Pennsylvania. In the end, Cyrus had agreed that Elijah could keep his secret for another three decades unless someone forced his hand, made him show his true colors.

All the digging the DEA had done, all the investigating by the state police, and they hadn't uncovered anything incriminating. The fire was suspicious. The fire marshal had no doubt that it was arson, but there was no proof that Elijah was involved. He'd been out of town, visiting an ailing family member when the sheds had gone up in flames.

A perfect alibi, but Cyrus knew he'd been involved, had planned the whole thing and probably paid someone a lot of money to do the job.

He followed Chance to the car, opened the door for Lark.

She smiled, the pink poodles on her shirt nearly glowing in the moonlight. "Thanks."

"Thank me after you're back in Baltimore, safe and sound," he muttered, and her smile broadened.

"Don't be a sore loser, Cyrus."

"That would be impossible, since I never lose," he responded lightly, and she laughed, the sound pealing through the quiet night.

It made him smile, and he was still smiling when he climbed into the passenger seat, met Chance's eyes.

"Stella and Boone are heading back to DC," Chance said. "I've asked Logan to meet us in River Fork. An extra man will give us an added advantage."

If that was supposed to make Cyrus feel better, it didn't. Logan Fitzgerald was a former marine, quick, smart and tough. But Elijah had already proven himself to be smart and determined. He was also a master manipulator. He'd been working hard to convince law enforcement that John had acted on his own, that he'd had hidden agendas, things that Elijah had known nothing about.

There had to be proof that he was lying.

They just had to find it.

He fingered the Bible he'd taken from Lark. There was something in it, a pattern of some sort. He was sure it was intentional. What he didn't know was if it was connected with Elijah.

"You have any connections with the CIA?" he asked, and Chance shot him a hard look.

"That's an interesting question."

"I think there might be a code in Joshua's Bible."

"Really?" Lark leaned over the seat, her head close to his, the scent of flowers and sunshine drifting from her hair.

"I can't be sure," he responded, taking a Maglite from the car's glove compartment and turning it on. He aimed the light on a page-marked section of scripture, eyeing the highlighted areas. "But I think there's a pattern here. I'm not familiar enough with coding to figure it out, but there are people who can."

"I might know a few," Chance said, a hint of interest in his voice. In the years that Cyrus had known him, Chance had never been anything but even keel. He didn't get overly emotional, didn't allow himself to be pulled into drama. He handled things with calm efficiency, worked as hard as any member of the team.

"How soon do you think you can get in touch with someone?"

"I should have someone lined up by tomorrow. As long as things don't go too far south today." He glanced in the rearview mirror, not a hint of concern or panic in his expression.

There was something, though, a little more tension in his hands as he held the steering wheel, a little more tautness in his jaw.

Cyrus glanced in the side mirror, watching the narrow country road. No cars. No lights. Nothing that should have been alarming.

"You see something?" he asked, and Chance frowned.

"Three flashes of light. Looked like headlights, but there's no road that way. Just the woods."

"Could be hunters."

"Not this close to a residential area, and not this early in the season."

"What are you thinking? A signal of some sort?"

"It doesn't make sense, but yeah. That's what I'm thinking."

"We've been here for five days. If Elijah knew it…" He'd have stayed away, waited until they left the safety of the house before he tried to grab Lark. "He'd have waited us out."

"We're thinking in the same direction," Chance said. "The guy has to be smart. He's been feeding people lies for decades and getting away with it. No way would he have tried to get at Lark while she was in the safe house. He'd wait until she was out in the open and vulnerable. Then he'd take his shot. Of course, those flashes could have been a hiker walking through the woods. Some teens out on an adventure."

"You don't believe that, and neither do I."

"You're right," Chance agreed. "We've got a choice to make. Stay the course or turn around."

"Stay the course," Lark said as if she really thought she had a choice.

"Sorry," Chance responded. "You don't get any say in it."

"I don't see—"

The headlights glinted on something in the woods. Just a brief second. Then gone. Not animal eyes. Something metal or glass.

Chance had seen it, too.

The car sped toward the end of the country road, its headlights suddenly off.

Something roared out of the woods behind them.

And Cyrus pulled his gun, opened the window.

"What are you doing?" Lark yelled. "You're going to get killed!"

He ignored her, focused on the lights of the oncoming vehicle. One shot, and it swerved.

Another and it slammed into a tree. A man jumped off, pulled a second from the vehicle.

Chance rounded a curve in the road, and the ATV was out of sight.

More lights flashed in the trees. More trouble coming.

Cyrus reloaded as another ATV sped into view.

"Get down and stay down," he shouted at Lark, and then he let loose with a volley of shots that sent the men in the ATV running for cover.

FOURTEEN

The car just kept going, bullets exploding, Lark praying, because there was nothing else she could do but cower in the backseat.

The car swerved, and she thought the tire must have been blown out. Chance kept it on the road, taking a sharp turn onto what she thought might be the highway. She didn't dare look.

Someone shouted, but she couldn't hear past the pulse of terror in her ears. She kept her head down, wrapped her arms around her knees. As if that would help if a bullet flew through the side of the car.

The car bounced over the road, and Lark braced herself for another barrage of bullets. It didn't come.

She waited, counting the seconds of silence, her mouth dry with fear, her skin tingling with adrenaline and terror.

Neither man spoke. No frantic call for help.

Nothing but the soft chug of the engine and the thump of the flat tire.

She lifted her head. They were definitely on the highway, the landscape whizzing by on either side as the car bounced along the road. Cyrus had settled back into his seat, was typing something into his cell phone.

"Are they gone?" she asked.

"For now," he responded, frowning as he looked at his cell phone. "Can I see your phone?"

She didn't ask why, just handed it over.

He pried open the back, his frown deepening. "That explains a lot."

"What?" She tried to see over the edge of the seat, tried to figure out what it was he was looking at.

"A tracking device." He lifted a small oblong object. "That made it really easy for them to find the safe house. They've probably been camping out in the woods, waiting for you to leave the house."

"Elijah must have pretty deep pockets to fund something like that," Chance said, pulling the car over to the side of the road.

"If he's been dealing in illegal weapons like that rocket launcher, that's not surprising," Cyrus responded.

Neither man seemed to be concerned about

the fact that they were sitting in a car waiting for Elijah's men to catch up to them.

Lark was.

She might be willing to go to River Fork, allow herself to bait the trap being set for Elijah, but she wasn't willing to be a sitting duck waiting for the bullet that would kill her.

"Shouldn't we be putting some distance between ourselves and them?" she asked, pivoting in her seat so she could see out the back window.

"We need new wheels," Chance responded. "Literally. There's no way we'll make it to River Fork in this."

"But—"

"They're long gone, Lark. There's no way they're hanging around waiting for the police to arrive. They took their shot at getting their hands on you, they failed. Now they're going to find a place to regroup," Cyrus cut in, handing her phone back. "I put my number in it."

"Seems a little unnecessary considering that she's about two feet from you," Chance said.

"She won't always be," Cyrus responded lightly. If he was embarrassed or annoyed by Chance's comment, it didn't show.

Lark shoved the phone into her pocket. "Thanks."

Cyrus smiled, glanced at his cell phone again. "Here they are. Let's move."

He and Chance opened their doors at exactly the same time, their movements almost perfectly in sync. No wasted motion from either of them.

Lights splashed across Cyrus's face as he opened Lark's door, tugged her out. Before her feet hit the ground, another car was behind theirs, and Boone was moving toward them, his long legs eating up the space.

"Two perps down," he said brusquely. "Non-life-threatening injuries, so the police may be able to get some information out of them."

"There were at least four," Cyrus responded, ushering Lark to the new vehicle, urging her into the backseat.

"Then two escaped. We found one ATV. Tire blown out, headlights smashed. Stella is keeping an eye on the perps. Police are on their way, so if you're going to go, now is a good time."

They were running from the police?

Lark didn't have time to ask the question. Before she could blink, her door was closed, and Cyrus was around the car, sliding into the seat beside her. He set Joshua's Bible in her lap, told her to buckle up.

Chance jumped into the front seat, started the engine and merged onto the road.

"Boone—?" she started, and Cyrus patted her thigh, his hand warm through the denim.

"He's staying with the car. The police will want to impound it."

"Aren't they also going to want to talk to us?"

"That's why we're taking off. We haven't committed a crime, so they can't legally hold us, but they can spend a lot of time asking questions. That's time we don't have." He tucked a strand of hair behind her ear, his fingers brushing her jaw. She shivered, fought the urge to lean her head against his shoulder, let herself soak in some of his warmth.

"I would think you'd be happy to stay here for a while," she said, looking away from his dark eyes, his strong face, because she was afraid of what she was feeling, afraid of where things were headed. She'd lost Joshua. She hadn't thought she would ever allow herself to care so deeply again. With Cyrus, she thought she *could* care that much. Thought that if she allowed herself to, she could fall into the gentleness of his touch, the darkness of his eyes, and lose herself there.

"I would be, but, if there's one thing I've learned, it's that it's always best to stick with the plan. A person starts veering left or right when he's supposed to go straight, and he just might find himself falling off a cliff."

That made her smile. "You're an interesting person, Cyrus."

"There are other words I'd use to describe him," Chance intoned, and Lark laughed.

"He's not the only one who'd use different words to describe me. There've been plenty of people who've said plenty of things about who I am," Cyrus said quietly. "But there's one thing I'm not, Lark, and that's fickle. I still don't want you in River Fork, but we're going there. You're going to follow the rules, do what you're told and stay safe, because that's part of the plan, too."

"That's good to know," she said, all her amusement gone, all her laughter dying away. "Because I'm not all that keen on dying."

He smiled, put an arm around her and pressed her head to his shoulder, his fingers tangling in the strands of hair near hear nape. "Are you keen on resting?"

She wasn't. Not really. She was too keyed up from the gunfight, too wound up from the adrenaline, but she didn't really want to move her head, so she nodded, closed her eyes and listened to the soft rumble of the men's conversation as the miles slipped away.

They made it to River Fork in just under three-and-a-half hours, pulling into the hospital parking lot a few minutes before eleven. There were no police cruisers waiting for them there. Cyrus thought that was a good sign. They'd taken a chance when they'd left Maryland, and he'd half expected to get pulled over before they crossed into Pennsylvania.

Chance pulled up in front of the hospital entrance, shifted in his seat, his gaze moving from Cyrus to Lark. She'd fallen asleep with her head against his shoulder, her hair spilling over her face.

"Is this going to cause problems?" he asked.

"No."

"Is it going to distract you?"

"I'd have told you if it was."

"You're sure? Because I really don't want to replace you."

"I'm sure."

He nodded, got out of the car without another word. Typical of Chance. He trusted his team, didn't second-guess them, didn't try to tell them how to run their personal lives. Didn't ever tell them not to get personally involved. Caring was the keystone of HEART. Without passion for the job, without a desperate need to rescue, reunite or bring closure, a team member was useless.

"Lark?" Cyrus brushed the hair off her cheek, surprised at how deeply involved he'd allowed himself to get. He could pull back. He knew it. Could keep going the way he had since Megan's death—passionate about the team's mission, but a little removed, a little detached.

He wouldn't pull back, though.

Not from Lark.

"Lark?" he said again, and she sat up straight, pure terror in her eyes and on her face.

"Are they back?"

"We're at the hospital," he responded, rubbing the tension from her shoulders, feeling her muscles relax again.

"The hospital. Right."

"We're going inside and straight to your father-in-law's room," he said, taking the Bible from her lap and sliding it under the seat. The SUV they were in was alarmed and would signal on Chance's key fob if anyone even touched it.

Cyrus would have preferred to take the Bible with him, but he didn't want Lark's in-laws to see it. They were hooked in deep with Elijah. He'd heard both of them waxing poetic about their religious leader.

"Sounds good." Lark yawned, reached for the door.

"Hold on," he said. "There are a couple of rules you need to follow. The first is that you stick close to either Chance or me. The second is—if I say *get down*, you're to do it. Immediately. No questions. No hesitation."

"We're at a hospital," she murmured, her cheeks pink from sleep, her eyes glassy. "Nothing is going to happen here."

"Let's hope you're right," he responded, getting out and rounding the car. He opened her door, took her elbow, Chance falling in behind them as he hurried her inside.

Eric Porter was on the third floor, and they took the elevator up, the canned music piped from the speaker doing nothing to improve Cyrus's mood. He was sticking to the plan for exactly the reason he'd given Lark, but he wasn't happy about it. He couldn't help feeling like he was sending her into enemy territory without any way to defend herself.

They reached Eric's room, and he walked in, not bothering to knock or to wait for an invitation. He wasn't expecting trouble, but that didn't mean he wasn't going to get it. Elijah was going to a lot of effort to get his hands on Lark. Cyrus was sure he'd put a price on her head, and he had a feeling it was a high one. They needed to take Elijah down, get him behind bars and put an end to this.

Whatever *this* was.

He frowned.

The Bible. He had a feeling that was the key,

that if they could figure out the code, they'd know exactly what Elijah was hiding.

He moved across the room, his gun holstered and hidden beneath his jacket. He didn't want to scare anyone, but no way was he going to give anyone an opportunity to harm Lark.

A woman sat beside the hospital bed. Mid-fifties. Very slender, hair pulled back in a tight bun. Maria Porter wore the uniform every Amos Way woman wore—long cotton skirt, thick long-sleeved sweater, sturdy shoes. No makeup, of course, but she had a gentle prettiness that made her look younger than she probably was.

Her eyes widened as he and Lark approached.

"Lark! You've returned!" she cried. There was no denying her excitement, but she moved slowly, easing up from her chair, walking sedately across the room. "Eric has been asking for you."

"Has he?" Lark embraced her mother-in-law, her gaze on the bed where Eric Porter lay.

Eyes closed, face slack, he didn't look anything like the man Cyrus had met at Amos Way. That man had been filled with energy and opinions, his gaze direct, his face hard. This man looked about a decade older. There were bandages on his arms and hands, bandages on the foot that peeked out from under a sheet, raw red flesh on his face.

"Of course," Maria said softly. "You know how much he cares about you."

Lark pulled a chair close to the bed, sat down and touched Eric's shoulder. "Dad?" she said. "How are you doing?"

Eric opened his eye, blinked as if he weren't quite sure of what he was seeing. "Lark?"

"That's right."

"How are you, my dear?" He lifted a bandaged hand and touched her shoulder. The move should have been fatherly, but it seemed more proprietary to Cyrus.

He had the urge to brush the hand away, step between the two, but Lark didn't seem bothered by the gesture. She smiled at her father-in-law. "Better than you, I'd say."

"That would not take much," he said, his gaze cutting to Cyrus. "I see the traitor is among us."

"Is that what I am?" he asked, leaning against the wall, not at all bothered by Eric's accusation.

"You know that you are," he responded, turning his head away.

As if he'd commanded her to, Maria did the same.

"I think you're being shunned," Chance

pointed out, his arms crossed over his chest, his shoulder against the doorjamb.

"What clued you in?"

"The fact that I'm the only one in the room who's willing to look at you."

"I'm willing," Lark said, her gaze fixed on her father-in-law.

"And yet you're not," Chance responded.

Lark didn't even crack a smile.

"How are you doing, Dad?" she asked. "Aside from the bandages and burns?"

"I will be better once the traitor leaves."

"I'm not going—"

A series of loud beeps cut him off. He knew what they were, what they meant. He met Chance's eyes. "The car," he said as if his boss could have mistaken the sound for something else.

Before he finished speaking, Chance was in the hall, racing toward the bank of elevators.

Cyrus strode to the window, looked out into the parking lot, Lark edging in close, her hair brushing his arm.

"What is it?" she whispered, her fear spilling out in those simple words.

"Someone trying to get into the car," he responded, scanning the nearly empty lot, finding Chance's car. No movement near it, but the alarm hadn't been triggered by nothing.

"Do you see anything?" Lark leaned toward the window, her forehead so close it nearly touched the glass. He imagined someone standing below, a high-powered rifle trained in their direction, and he moved between her and the glass.

"Move away from the window," he said calmly, his heart tripping at the thought of her lying in a pool of her own blood.

She didn't balk, didn't question. Just returned to her seat, sat there tensely. The silence of the room seemed to have a pulse of its own, its loudness filling Cyrus's head. He wasn't surprised that Maria wasn't asking questions, but Eric's muteness was out of character.

Did he know something?

Had he or someone let Elijah know that they'd arrived?

He didn't have time to ask. A shadow moved at the edge of the lot, ducked under some trees that stood there. Not enough foliage to offer cover, but it put something between him and the parking lot.

Seconds later, another figure stepped into view.

Chance for sure. Cyrus recognized the quick stride and confident carriage. He pulled out his cell phone, dialed Chance's number, waiting impatiently for his boss to pick up.

One ring. Two. Three. Four.

Finally, Chance answered.

"Go ahead," he said by way of greeting.

"Someone walked into the trees to your left."

"I saw him."

"You're going in after him or coming back up?"

"Checking on the car and coming up. They divide us, and it's going to be easier to conquer us. Logan is on the way. ETA five minutes. We leave as soon as he gets here. Make sure Lark knows it, and make sure she's not going to give us any grief about it. I don't like the way things feel, and the sooner we find a place to hole up, the happier I'm going to be." Chance disconnected.

"Is everything okay?" Lark asked quietly.

"We're going to be leaving in about five minutes." He touched her shoulder, eyed Eric. The man's burns weren't faked, but his quiet demeanor, his silence, that wasn't indicative of his character. Even wounded, even in pain.

"Did you contact someone after we got here, Eric?" he asked, and the man turned his head, refused to look at Cyrus.

"Did you?" Cyrus pressed.

"I would never betray my family the way you betrayed your friendships," Eric responded.

"That's not an answer."

"It is an answer. Just not the one you want," Eric responded. "If you want a different one, I will give you this. You look at my hands and tell me how I could have contacted anyone without being seen. Then ask the question again."

There were ways, but Cyrus couldn't pull back the covers, search for a hidden cell phone.

"Eric," Lark said, lifting his bandaged hand. "What do you know about Joshua's death?"

The question surprised Cyrus. It must have shocked Eric. He sat up, the sheet falling away. Bandages wrapped around his chest, covering him from armpit to waist, but he looked to be more filled with anger than with pain.

"What kind of question is that?" he demanded, yanking his hand from Lark's.

"One that I want an answer to. You knew your son better than almost anyone. You know how careful he was with his guns."

"Even careful people make mistakes," Eric said, his face pale beneath the burns.

"Not Joshua. Not about this," Lark insisted. "Did you know there was a note on the table near his body?"

Eric pressed his lips together, but didn't answer.

"You did know," she breathed. "Why didn't you tell me?"

"He didn't want you to be hurt," Maria answered, her words shaky. "He didn't want you to suffer the way we were suffering. Our son. Taking his own life." Her voice broke, and she buried her face in her hands.

"Enough!" Eric barked. "We will not discuss this further. You have to go, so leave," he said. "But go with my blessing, and know that I care about you. Even if you have betrayed the trust of our family."

"I have never betrayed you."

"You took something that didn't belong to you. You have kept it from the person who owns it. That makes you a thief, Lark. You are our daughter. Your sin is our sin."

"Eric—"

"Will you deny it?"

"Yes."

"Then you are a liar, too. Your sin seeped into our peaceful lives. Your lies became ours, and my son became a victim of them."

"What are you talking about?" Lark looked stricken, her eyes deep gray in her pale face.

"Say your goodbyes to Mother and to me, and then go. I wish you well." He held out his hand, and she took it, leaning down to kiss his cheek.

"Goodbye, Eric," she murmured, and he nodded, turning his face away.

Maria stood and hugged Lark, whispering something in her ear. There was something in her face, something in her gaze that made Cyrus's pulse pick up a notch.

"Go in peace," she finally said, stepping back, squeezing both Lark's hands and releasing them.

That was it.

Simple. To the point.

She sat, lowering her head as if she were praying, dismissing Lark the same way Eric had.

It had to hurt, but Lark kept her chin up, her emotions in check as Cyrus took her arm and led her into the hall.

FIFTEEN

The note in Lark's hand felt as big as an ocean liner but it was only a small square of folded paper. She wanted to open it, see what her mother-in-law had passed to her, but Maria's whispered words echoed in her head.

We are in danger. You must be very careful. Elijah is watching your every move. Don't tell anyone about this. Do not let the traitor see what I am giving you. If you do, we will die.

The words had surprised her, but Maria's terror had been real, her hands shaking as she'd squeezed Lark's, pressed the scrap of paper into her palm.

"Cyrus!" someone called, and she looked up the hall, her pulse racing, that little piece of paper heavy as a two-ton weight. She shoved it in her pocket as a blond-haired man strode toward them.

"Took you long enough," Cyrus muttered, offering a hand to the man. "Logan Fitzgerald, this is Lark Porter. Lark, Logan is a member of HEART. He's also a former marine. I try not to hold that against him."

She tried to smile, but her lips were stiff, her muscles uncooperative.

"It's nice to meet you, Logan," she managed to say, and the blond smiled, his dark blue eyes sharp and assessing.

"I hear you've been through some tough times."

"Yes," she said, the word catching on the back of her throat, that little scrap of paper taunting her.

Don't tell anyone about this.

A month ago, she wouldn't have. A week ago, she might not have. Three months ago, she'd been foolish enough to think she could bring Elijah down on her own, that somehow, by the sheer strength of her determination, she'd be able to outsmart a man who had manipulated and tricked an entire community.

She'd been wrong then.

Would she be wrong now?

If she kept the note secret? If she found somewhere to read it without anyone seeing? Would that be a mistake?

"We're going to change that," Logan continued. "Pretty soon, you'll be safe and back to your old life."

Her old life?

It's what she'd thought she'd wanted, what she'd been longing for during the endless months that she'd been held in Amos Way. When she'd been a prisoner in the trailer, she'd wanted nothing more than to go back to Baltimore, live in her empty apartment, continue her life without the deep connections that she'd once had with Joshua.

It was too hard to love someone and lose them.

Too difficult to care so deeply and have to say goodbye.

But right then, she thought the hardest thing of all, the most difficult thing, would be to never have experienced the kind of love she and Joshua had shared.

Taking a chance on something like that? She thought it might be worth any heartache it would bring, that it might be worth any sorrow.

She met Cyrus's eyes, could see the questions there.

He knew. Not that she'd been given the note, but that she was hiding something.

He didn't say anything, just cupped her elbow, moved her through the hall. Chance met them at the elevator, and they rode down in silence, that piece of paper between Lark and the men who were trying to save her.

It was that more than anything else that made her decide.

Cyrus had risked everything for her. Chance had put his life on hold to play bodyguard. Both men had proven to be invaluable allies. Logan had dropped whatever he'd been doing, left DC, made the trip to help his comrades. Because they'd asked, and because she'd needed it. She'd be a fool to keep going the direction she always had, to keep pushing to do things her way, to solve her problems alone.

"She gave me something," she said, her voice so loud, it nearly startled her.

Cyrus smiled, the warmth in his eyes, in his face, making her heart reach for his, her body lean toward his.

"I was wondering when you were going to tell us," he said, his fingers caressing her arm, their warmth easing some of the chill that had settled in her bones.

"She said that Elijah is watching. That she and Eric will be killed if he knows you've seen the note."

"A note, huh?" Chance led the way off the elevator. "You read it yet?"

"No."

"We'll look at it in the car. I called Sheriff Johnson. He wants us to come to the station. He can put us up there for a few nights."

"Hopefully not in a jail cell," Logan muttered. "I spent a few too many days in one while I was in Mexico."

"I told you not to mess with the local PD," Chance said, pausing at the door. "You want to get your car, Logan? I think that's a better option than mine."

"The Bible—" she began.

"Right here." He patted his coat. "I grabbed it after I searched the car for explosives."

"Find anything?" Cyrus asked.

Lark was too busy thinking about the possibility of a car bomb going off to ask questions.

"Another tracking device planted under the license plate. I don't think they wanted to risk killing Lark. Not before they got what they wanted from her."

"Sounds like you've got some serious trouble here," Logan said. "I like it."

He jogged outside, and Cyrus shook his head. "That guy has some serious adrenaline junkie issues."

"He's a good team player," Chance responded, taking Lark's other arm as a dark Jeep pulled up in front of the entrance. "Ready? Let's move!"

Seconds later, she was buckled in, sandwiched between Cyrus and Chance as Logan sped from the parking lot and headed toward the sheriff's department.

"Might as well take out that note now," Chance said as they headed up Main Street.

She reached into her pocket, her hand shaking as she pulled out the folded paper. She tried to unfold it, but she couldn't find the edges, couldn't quite get it to open.

Probably because of her shaky hands, her trembling body.

She wanted to read the note, and she didn't.

Because whatever it said, it was a message from Elijah. She was sure of that, certain that her in-laws had been ordered to give it to her.

"Let me." Chance took it from her hand, unfolded it easily.

He took a small Maglite from his coat pocket, handed it and the note to Lark. "Go ahead."

She turned on the light, aimed the beam at a two-by-two scrap of writing paper.

The words were written in bold black ink, the letters tiny and precise.

> You have what I want. Bring it to me, or the Porters die. Men first. Women second. Children third. Not in one day, but over time, so that each suffers more than the next. Their blood on your hands.

There was an address beneath the words. No signature, but she knew who'd written it. Elijah.

"What's it say?" Logan asked as he pulled into the police department.

She wanted to answer, but the words caught in her throat, fear holding them captive. There was no doubt in her mind that Elijah would follow through on his threat.

Cyrus read the note instead, his voice ringing out into the quiet Jeep, the words echoing in Lark's head, filling her with terror as Logan parked the car and they headed in to meet with the sheriff.

"No," Cyrus said for the thousandth time. He could probably say it a thousand times more and get the same response. Silence.

"You can ignore me all you want," he continued. "But that won't change anything. I don't like the plan. We need to come up with a different one."

"I suppose you have a suggestion?" Sheriff Johnson asked, a topographical map spread out on the desk in front of him.

Cyrus didn't. That was the problem.

The plan they'd come up with made sense—send a team to the specified location, have them move in silently, surround the abandoned ski resort before Lark drove in. Once she arrived, they'd wait for Elijah to make a move, and then they'd tighten the net and bring him in.

There was only one problem with that. Cyrus didn't want Lark anywhere near Elijah. He didn't care how many men and women were in position beforehand. He didn't care how many or how well trained they were. All he cared about was keeping her safe.

"My suggestion is that we come up with a new plan."

"*My* suggestion is," Lark said, pushing away from the desk and the map and getting to her feet, "that we go for it."

"Go for what?" he demanded. "Your death?"

"Elijah isn't going to kill me until he gets what he wants," she replied.

"That does not," he growled, "make me feel better."

"This isn't about you," Logan cut in. "It's about Lark. It's about her husband's death. It's about something else, something that is probably a lot bigger than any of that. A rocket launcher? Dude, that's serious weaponry. You said that shipments were coming in and out of the compound every week. That's potentially thousands of those things. They weren't in the sheds when they were burned down, so where are they?"

"We aren't completely sure they were ever

there," Sheriff Johnson said. "We haven't found any evidence on the compound yet."

"Come on!" Logan scoffed. "Everything that's happened is pointing to some kind of trafficking ring. Weapons make sense in light of the rocket launcher that was used. For all you know, this guy is a lunatic and trying to usher in the apocalypse. He's got to be stopped."

There was a heartbeat of silence after he finished, and then the room exploded with noise. Sheriff Johnson reiterating how important it was to stop his half brother, but how careful they needed to be to not jump to conclusions. Chance asking how many men and women Johnson could round up for the mission. Logan on his cell phone, asking for more HEART presence.

All of it swirling around Cyrus, but he was only partially aware of it.

He knew…

Of course he knew.

That Logan was right.

Elijah had to be stopped at any cost. He just didn't want that cost to be Lark.

He met her eyes, and she smiled.

"God is in control, right?" she said quietly, but he heard the words more loudly than any of the others, felt them more deeply.

"Right," he said.

"So, you've got nothing to worry about."

"I'm still going to worry."

"But, you're going to support me in this, right?" she asked, her gaze somber, her face pale. "Because I have to do it. There's no choice. No other option. If the police go to the ski lodge and find Elijah there, he'll deny the note, he'll insist that he had nothing to do with it."

"I know." He did, and he knew that Elijah would have made sure there was no evidence to the contrary, no way to trace the note to him.

"Then say you're going to back me, Cyrus." Her voice broke, and she took his hand, her palm cool and dry against his. "Because, I can't do it without you."

That was all it took.

Just those words, and he couldn't deny her.

He didn't like the plan, didn't want the plan, but for Lark, he'd follow through on it.

"All right," he said. "I'll back you."

She smiled at that, turning back to the desk, to the map, but not letting go of his hand.

Chance noticed, his gaze dropping for a fraction of a second, settling on that place where Cyrus's and Lark's hands were linked.

He met Cyrus's eyes, nodded and then leaned over the desk, pointed to a flagged area.

"This," he said, "is where HEART will go in."

That was it. The beginning of the plan that Cyrus had committed to. No backing out now. No changing course. All he could do was follow through and pray that when it was over, Lark would still be standing.

SIXTEEN

Three in the morning.

Never a good time to be out and about.

Lark was about to be both.

She moved through the dark room, easing around a desk as she tugged on her sweater, shoved her cell phone in her pocket.

"You're sure you want to do this?" Cyrus asked, tugging her hair out from her collar.

"No," she admitted, smoothing her hand down the thick cotton shirt she'd been asked to wear. She could feel the wires that were taped to her skin, but she'd been assured by a female officer that they weren't visible.

"If you want to back out," Cyrus said, buttoning both cardigan buttons, "I'll support you."

"Support me? You'll throw a party and dance a jig," she joked, her stomach churning with anxiety and dread.

As much as she wanted to go through with the plan, she was terrified of facing Elijah alone.

Not alone, she reminded herself. *Thirty people are already in the woods waiting for you.*

Five members of HEART, fifteen local and state police. DEA agents.

And Cyrus would be there.

He'd wait until she drove away, then he'd take a back road into the ski resort, walk through some heavy woods to get to the crumbling lodge.

Lark had seen pictures of the place, had spent three hours learning every aspect of the plan.

She knew who would be where, what their responses to any given situation would be.

She was still terrified.

The way she saw things, she'd be a fool not to be.

"You're right about the party, but I've never been all that great of a dancer," Cyrus responded, smiling through the darkness, his eyes gleaming.

Once he'd committed to the plan, he'd gone in wholeheartedly. No hesitation. No holding back. He'd helped mark coordinates and flag the map. He knew what they were getting into. Probably a lot better than Lark did. His calmness eased some of her fear, but it couldn't ease it all.

"Really? I'm shocked. I thought you were good at everything you did."

He chuckled, pulling her in close, leaning down so they were eye to eye. "For the record, Lark, I admire your choice. It's one I would have made."

"I know."

"Do you also know that I'm not planning to say goodbye when this is over?"

"*If* this is over," she responded, her heart beating frantically. Not from fear this time. From him. His presence. His words. The softness of his face as he looked into her eyes.

"It will be, and when it is, we're both going to be free to go back to what we were before it happened, go back to our lives and live them just exactly the same way we did before. If that's what you want." He cupped her face in his hands, his palms cool against her suddenly warm cheeks. "I'm hoping it isn't."

There was so much she could have said, so many fears she could have shared. So many worries about losing her heart again, having it broken again.

But time was ticking away. Elijah was waiting, the plan playing out the way it was supposed to, so she kept it simple, said what she had to and nothing more. "It isn't."

He smiled, brushing her lips with his, the kiss so sweet, so tender, her heart broke from it.

A single tear slipped down her cheek. A tear for what she'd lost, and for what she was about to gain.

"No tears," he said quietly, brushing the moisture from her face, kissing her again, deeply, passionately, and she wanted to cling to him, forget the mission and Elijah and the work they still had to do to bring him down.

He backed away, his breathing ragged.

"It's time," he said simply, and she knew it was.

He handed her a thick leather manual that Sheriff Johnson had had in his office. Joshua's Bible had been locked up in a safe. Would be kept there until one of Chance's contacts could come for it.

She walked to the window, shoved it open, climbed out, dropping to the ground, the manual clutched in her clammy hand, Cyrus's kiss still on her lips.

Logan had parked in the front of the building, and she moved in that direction, keeping to the shadows, because that's what she'd have done if she were really sneaking away.

She thought she felt a dozen eyes watching as she unlocked the Jeep's door and shoved the keys in the ignition.

Her hands shook, but she managed to steer the vehicle onto the road, wind her way through town and out onto a narrow country road.

She knew the way. It had been drilled into her by Logan, by Chance, by Cyrus.

She touched her lips, was sure they were still warm from his kiss.

She wanted what the future would bring, wanted to explore what life would be like with Cyrus in it.

That didn't mean letting go of her memories, it didn't mean forgetting what she'd had with Joshua. It simply meant moving on. It was what Joshua would have wanted for her, what she would have wanted for him if she'd been the one to die.

Tears burned the back of her eyes.

She blinked them away.

She had to stay focused on the mission, stick to the plan.

She had twenty minutes to make it to the ski lodge. One minute after that, and she was supposed to be engaging with Elijah, trying to get him to reveal his secrets.

That was the part she had no control over.

Don't veer from the course.

She could almost hear Cyrus whispering in her ear as she drove up a steep hill, turned onto a rutted road. The woods were deep here, the road meandering upward through endless trees. There should be thirty people hidden in the darkness, slowly making their way to the abandoned ski lodge.

Should be?

Were.

She wasn't alone.

She just had to keep reminding herself of that.

The road opened up again, spilling out into a cleared area dotted with cabins, tangled with overgrown weeds.

She passed the remnants of a small lodge, knew she was closing in on the main lodge. Her stomach twisted, her heart beating so fast, she thought it might jump from her chest.

There! Right up ahead. The main lodge. Windows boarded up. Porch roof caving in. Door yawning open. It looked like every child's worst nightmare.

She parked the Jeep ten yards away, allowing plenty of room for the team to move in. Thirty seconds, and she was supposed to be at the door, knocking.

Only the door was open, and she was sure Elijah was in the darkness beyond, peering out at her.

Please, Lord, she whispered as she opened the door. *Help me do this.*

And then she was out of the Jeep and moving toward the lodge, the manual clutched to her chest.

"Why have you come?" The voice came from somewhere beyond the doorway.

His voice.

Elijah's.

She felt it shivering along her spine, lodging in her chest.

She could barely breathe from the weight of it, but she kept moving.

"I said," Elijah hissed, "why have you come?"

She was less than two feet from the porch steps, Cyrus's words ringing through her head.

A person starts veering left or right when he's supposed to go straight, and he just might find himself falling off a cliff.

She knew the plan. Step by step. Second by second. Get to the door, force Elijah out onto the wide front porch. The team would have a clear shot of him there.

"I have what you want," she responded, moving closer, a warning whispering through her head.

He'd known she was coming. Just like they'd expected he would, but he didn't seem eager to get what she was carrying, didn't demand that she hand it over.

"What I want," he responded, his voice emotionless, "is what I deserve."

"What's that?" she asked, taking another step, her foot on the bottom stair, something deep inside telling her to stop.

"I am heir to the kingdom that will be ushered in with fire and brimstone," he intoned, the words chilling her to the bone.

Get him talking. Keep him talking.

The words raced through her head, the plan crystal clear in her mind.

She didn't want to follow it. She wanted to run into the woods and hide from a man who was obviously crazy.

"Is that why you killed Joshua? Because he discovered your plan?"

"It is not my plan. It is God's plan. Your husband is dead because he interfered with it."

"Did he know he was going to die?" she asked, the questions slipping out, her voice cracking.

"Everyone knows he is going to die, Lark." He chuckled, and she saw something move in the doorway. A hint of a shadow nothing more.

"*Everyone* is not murdered, and that's what you did. You murdered him."

"I did not pull the trigger, if that's what you're saying."

"Then you had John do it."

"John was too much of a coward to do the Lord's will. In the end, it is what killed him. Bring me what you have," he demanded.

"Tell me who killed my husband," she countered.

"Someone who believes in me, who knows I am the new messiah. Someone very close to Joshua," he added, those sly last words the only ones that mattered.

She thought about her father-in-law, the one man in the compound Joshua had trusted completely.

"Not Eric," she said, the words barely above a whisper.

He heard, his laughter drifting out of the darkness, wrapping around her heart. "He will receive his reward when I possess what is rightfully mine."

"What is that?" she asked, her body shaking, her thoughts scattering in a thousand different directions.

Not Eric.

Not his own father.

"My kingdom." And suddenly he was there, out on the porch, dressed in a long white tunic, his hand reaching for her. "Bring me what Joshua took, and I will let your family live."

"I don't have any family," she responded, the words ringing hollowly through the silent morning. Not a sound from the woods. No scurry of animals. No crackle of leaves. Not even a breeze moved through the treetops.

Was the team there?

Was Cyrus?

Stick to the plan.

But she couldn't make herself walk up those steps.

"We are all one family," he intoned, and she cringed, her mind recoiling from his obvious insanity.

"If you want what I have, come and get it," she said, backing away, trying to force him farther into the open.

"A book. Is that what you're holding? Is that where he hid it?"

"Hid what?"

"The information he stole from me. Joshua was very smart. He could have done so much for my kingdom. Instead, he betrayed me. He stole from me. He tried to stop me from having what is mine."

They were back at that again, and she almost stepped forward, handed him the manual just so she could be done with it. Only she didn't think he planned to be done.

She took another step back.

There was something in his left hand, and

she squinted trying to see through the darkness. Not a gun. Not a knife. A remote of some sort.

And then, she knew exactly what he'd planned, knew just how crazy he was.

No time for the plan. No time to think of a new one either.

She had to act, and she threw the manual, tossing it onto the porch a few feet from where Elijah stood.

Then she ran toward the trees, her feet like leaden weights, her body seeming to move in slow motion. A hundred yards from the house, and it wasn't enough. She knew it, knew she was out of time.

Someone rushed from the woods, tackled her to the ground, and the world exploded, fire shooting into the sky, hot air washing over her. She was rolling, an arm locked around her waist, a hand over her head.

Cyrus, she wanted to say, but the words were swept into a blackness so deep, she didn't think she'd ever escape from it.

SEVENTEEN

"She's coming to," someone said, the words finding their way into the darkness, pulling her from oblivion and into pain so intense she groaned.

"She probably wishes she wasn't," someone responded, the feminine voice familiar.

She forced her eyes open, stared into a bright green gaze and a pale pretty face. Stella.

"Cyrus—" she tried to say, the words rasping, her throat raw.

"Alive," Stella responded, leaning closer and peering into Lark's eyes. "Looks like your brains weren't too scrambled. The doctors were worried."

"*You* were worried," Boone scoffed from a chair next to the bed. "She's been pacing around here for three hours, muttering under her breath."

"I don't mutter," Stella responded. "And I

don't worry. I knew she was going to be fine. How are you feeling, Lark?"

"Like I was hit by a train," she responded truthfully, trying to sit up.

"Here." Stella sighed, pressing a button so the head of the bed rose. "Better?"

"Yes. Thanks."

"Drink." Stella handed her a plastic cup of water. "Little sips. You've got a couple of broken ribs. If you puke, your body is not going to be happy."

She took a sip of water, placed the cup on a small table, wincing as she moved. "Where is Cyrus? I need to see him."

"Probably giving the doctors a hard time. He has a broken clavicle and a cracked wrist. He also has a bad attitude when he's hurt."

"I need to see him," she repeated.

"Not going to happen," Stella responded. "He's a floor up, and you're not in any shape to go there."

"Says who?"

"The doctor."

"He hasn't said it to me." She eased her legs over the side of the bed, pain wrapping around her chest, squeezing her breath away. She ignored it, ignored the cold sweat that beaded her brow.

"There is no way," Stella began, but a commotion in the hall stopped her short. A woman's voice. A man's. Both of them raised.

Seconds later, Cyrus was in the doorway, a nurse on one side of him, Chance on the other. Jeans torn and covered with soot and blood, arm in a sling, his eyes blazed with irritation and anger, his gaze sweeping over Boone and Stella and settling on Lark.

"Thank the Lord," he whispered, all the fire fading from his eyes as he limped across the room, lowered himself onto the edge of the bed.

"Are you okay?" He touched her cheek, his fingers slipping to her shoulder and settling there.

"I think I'm better than you," she responded.

"I'm fine."

"Stella said you broke your clavicle and cracked your wrist. I don't think that's fine."

"Stella," he said, shooting his coworker a hard look, "has a big mouth."

"I have an honest mouth. Which, now that I'm thinking about it, is parched." She grabbed Boone's arm, dragged him toward the door. "Come on. I'm sure you're hungry. Let's go to the cafeteria."

"You think they've got chicken pot pie there?" he asked as he stepped out into the hall. "That's what Scout is making for dinner tonight, and I've got a feeling I'm going to miss it."

Whatever else he said was lost as they disappeared down the hall. The nurse followed, apparently unwilling to deal with Cyrus any longer.

"Well," Chance said, pulling a chair over and sitting next to the bed. "You got what you wanted, Cyrus. You're in her room. You can see she's alive. Happy?"

"Very," he responded. "I'll be even happier when I know that we've got the coordinates for Elijah's weapons stores."

"My CIA friend arrives in an hour. She'll take a look at the Bible," Chance said. "I don't think we'll need it. Now that Elijah…" He glanced at Lark.

"Is dead?" she said. "I know he is. You don't have to tiptoe around it."

"You've been through a lot, Lark. I don't want to add more to it."

"What more could there be?" She tried to grab the water, but her hands were shaking so much, it sloshed over the side.

"Here." Cyrus took it from her hand, held it while she took a sip.

"Thanks," she said, and he smiled into her eyes, ran his thumb along her jaw.

"You're going to have a big bruise there."

"Not as big as the one on your shoulder."

"It will heal," he responded. "You'll heal," he added.

"I know." She took his hand, wove her fingers through his, not caring that Chance was there, watching them both, frowning slightly.

"Your father-in-law is in custody, Lark. You need to know that," Chance said quietly. "He's still in the hospital, but the police have a guard stationed at his room. As soon as he's released, he'll be taken to jail. Sheriff Johnson has already questioned him. At first he wouldn't talk." He ran a hand down his jaw. "Then we showed him some photos of Elijah's body. Not pleasant, but he needed to see them. He didn't believe Elijah could die. He'd been sure that no amount of fire, no explosion, no bullet could take his leader's life. When he saw that he was wrong…" He shook his head.

"Poor Eric," she said, because she really was sorry for him. Sorry for the lies he'd believed, for the false faith he'd lived. For what he'd done in the name of that faith.

She thought of Joshua, so alive and vibrant, so filled with true faith, and she wanted to cry for what had been lost.

"I'm sorry," Cyrus said, gently squeezing her hand.

"Me, too. Do you think…?" She didn't finish the question, didn't have the heart to ask it.

"That Joshua knew his father shot him?" Cyrus spoke softly, his thumb skimming her wrist, the caress offering comfort that she desperately needed. "I've seen the autopsy reports. The bullet went through Joshua's temple. He probably died before any of what was happening registered."

That didn't make it better, but she was glad. Glad that Joshua hadn't known that final betrayal.

"According to Eric," Chance said, "he didn't pull the trigger. John did. We'll probably never know the truth. What we do know is that Elijah was a fanatic with a history of drug abuse. He was arrested twice in his early teens. Both times for possession and distribution of cocaine. The records were sealed, and Sheriff Johnson had to get an injunction to open them. He received the file this morning."

"That was a long time ago," Cyrus said.

"It was, but a K-9 team found traces of cocaine in Elijah's house. I think he was still an addict, probably delusional from too many years doing hard-core drugs."

"That doesn't make it better," Lark said.

"No, but it gives the FBI and DEA some insight into what was going on. Eric said that Elijah had planned tonight carefully, put enough explosives in that lodge to bring it down. He'd assured Eric that that was the beginning of the apocalypse. That you would be killed and reap the rewards of your betrayal, and that Elijah would walk away unscathed."

"Do you think Elijah really believed that?"

"He blew himself up," Chance said. "So, I'd say he did. Thankfully, he didn't take either of you out while he did it. Now, if you'll excuse me, I've got to go smooth things over with that nurse. She wasn't happy about your escape, Cyrus." He walked from the room.

"I'm sorry," Lark said as soon as he was gone, because she had to get it off her chest, had to say what she'd been thinking.

"For what?" Cyrus asked, the bruise on his shoulder so deep black and purple it hurt to look at.

"I did exactly what you told me not to do. I changed the plan, and I nearly got us killed."

He shook his head, smiled that smile that she'd grown to love. "I think," he said, his hand moving up her arm, cupping her cheek, "that you need to stop carrying so much guilt around, Lark."

"It's not guilt. It's fact. I—"

"Assessed the situation and made a split-second decision that saved your life. I'd much rather be sitting here in the hospital with you, both of us bruised and broken, than be sitting in my DC apartment alone, thinking about everything we might have had together."

"I still—"

He leaned in, stopping the last few words with his lips. Just a gentle kiss, one so light and tender she nearly cried with the beauty of it.

"Will you be doing that every time you want me to be quiet?" she asked, and he laughed.

"Only if you want me to."

"I think I might," she responded, and he kissed her palm, folded her fingers over the warmth that lingered there.

"You know what I think, Lark?"

"What?" she asked, her ribs aching, her body sore, but her heart at peace.

"That the next few months and years are going to be interesting. Wait here. I'm going to find that nurse, find you some clothes and then I'm going to break us out of here. I don't know about you, but I've had just about all I can take of River Fork, Pennsylvania."

She was smiling as he walked out of the room, still smiling when Stella entered, muttering under her breath as she helped Lark into clothes, lectured her about the idiocy of leaving the hospital too soon.

Lark ignored her, because she wanted out of River Fork as much as Cyrus did, and because she was ready to finally move on.

"Ready?" Cyrus appeared in the doorway, clean shirt pulled over his chest, his arm still cradled in the sling, a soft cast covering his wrist.

"Yes," she responded, smiling into his eyes as she took his hand and let him lead her out of the hospital and into their future.

EPILOGUE

Essex had very loud children.

That was something Lark had known before she'd agreed to babysit. What she hadn't known was just how much of a mess four young children could make.

She eyed the toys strewn across the living room floor, the pillows tossed from the couch. It would have been a good idea to have the kids help clean up before she tucked them into bed.

Too little too late.

Five hours of high-level exuberant play had tired everyone out. By the time she'd finished reading the last bedtime story, every one of the kids was asleep.

Essex would be pleased.

It was his anniversary, and he wanted Janet to have a nice relaxing evening. Dinner. A movie. Maybe a walk near the inner harbor. He'd sketched the plan out for Lark, asked her opinion on the restaurant, the flowers he should buy, the gift—a pretty necklace with a diamond encrusted heart pendant.

He was going all out, and Lark wasn't going to ruin it by having the couple come home to a house that looked like a tornado had struck.

She glanced at her cell phone as she grabbed toys and tossed them into a bin that stood against the wall.

No message from Cyrus.

She hadn't really been expecting one, but she'd been hoping.

He'd left town a week ago, heading to Mexico to find a child who'd been kidnapped by a non-custodial parent. It was his fourth mission in the seven months since they'd been dating. She was getting used to the routine—taking him to the airport, kissing him goodbye, telling him to be careful and then watching him walk through the security gate at the airport.

It never got easier, but she wouldn't complain. Cyrus was doing what God had called him to do. She'd never stand in the way of that.

But she sure missed him when he was gone. More each time he left.

Because every day that she was with him, every moment that they spent together, she found something more to like about him.

She grabbed a pillow, tossed it onto the couch.

She missed Joshua, too. That wouldn't ever

stop, but she'd learned to move on. Knowing that Elijah was gone, that he was no longer a threat, made that easier. The DEA had found storage units in towns all over the United States. Each stacked with illegal firearms and weapons. The Bible had been the key to locating the caches, and Eric had been key to understanding Elijah's mindset. With his leader gone, he'd crumbled, admitting that he'd killed Ethan to make sure nothing got in the way of Elijah's plan.

He hadn't admitted to killing Joshua.

Lark wasn't sure she believed his denial.

At this point, it didn't matter. Eric was in prison, probably for the rest of his life. Amos Way was closed down, some of the people living peacefully in River Fork.

Keys rattled outside the front door, and she snagged the last pillow, tossing it onto the couch as the door opened.

Essex and his wife stepped in, both of them smiling.

"How did it go?" Janet asked. "Did they drive you nuts?"

"They were great," she answered honestly. "How about Essex? Did he drive you nuts?"

Janet laughed, and Essex scowled, the humor in his eyes obvious.

"Now is that any way to speak to a man who brought you a surprise?" he asked.

"A surprise?"

"A big one," he replied. "Picked it up at the airport on my way here."

"Airport?"

"And I'll tell you what," he continued without answering her question. "It was driving me nuts with all its worrying about you and bugging me about you and telling me to—"

"Shut up?" Cyrus asked, stepping into the house, his hair ruffled, his eyes deeply shadowed.

She didn't hesitate, didn't wait, didn't do anything but throw herself into his arms.

"You're home!" she cried, cupping his face, looking into his eyes.

"Almost," he responded. "I was hoping you could give me a ride back to my place."

"I'd give you a ride to the end of the earth if you asked me to," she replied, and he laughed.

"Good to know, but I think I'm a little too tired for that long of a trip."

"You should have called me when you got in, the kids and I could have picked you up."

"I could have, but Essex and I had a plan, and I always stick to my plans."

"Plan for what?" she asked, confused but

not really caring. He was there. That was all that mattered.

"This," he replied, pulling a small box from his pocket.

"What—?"

"Be quiet and listen to the man," Essex said.

"Yes," Cyrus said with a laugh. "Listen to the man, because I want this done right, and I'm a little tired. I may not remember the speech Essex helped me write."

"Essex helped you write speech?" she asked, her heart racing.

"I didn't want to forget anything important. Like telling you how much you mean to me, how deeply I love you."

"How glad you are that I brought the two of you together," Essex added and Janet shushed him.

"That, too," Cyrus responded as he stared straight into Lark's eyes.

She couldn't look away, didn't want to.

Not even when he opened the box, revealing a beautiful sapphire ring.

"I thought about getting you a diamond, but that seemed too ordinary for someone as special as you. You are everything I didn't know I was looking for, Lark, everything I didn't dare dream I could have. When I leave town, I want to know I'm coming home to you. When

I come home, I want to spend every minute by your side. Will you marry me?"

She nodded, because she couldn't speak past the lump in her throat, couldn't see past the tears in her eyes.

All the hardship and heartbreak and difficulties had led her to this place and this man and this life. She was so very grateful for that.

He put the ring on her finger, pulled her into his arms, kissing her with tenderness until Essex cleared his throat and Janet said she'd made a cake for the occasion.

Cyrus backed away but didn't release her.

"Does cake sound good?" he asked, and she smiled through her tears.

"Anything sounds good if you're part of it."

"Good, great," Essex interrupted. "Enough of the mushy stuff. Janet makes a mean chocolate cake, and I've been waiting all day to dig into it."

Lark laughed at that, grabbing Cyrus's hand and tugging him toward the kitchen, her heart filled with joy for what they would build together.

* * * * *

Dear Reader,

God is always with us. Sometimes, when we are hardest hit and in the deep pit of terrible circumstances, it is easy to forget that.

Lark Porter has never had it easy. She's climbed her way out of a terrible childhood, met a wonderful man, fallen in love. Her marriage should have been idyllic, but when her husband dies under suspicious circumstances, all that she's put her faith and trust in seems to crumble. Cyrus Mitchell doesn't want a committed relationship, but when an old army buddy asks him to make sure Lark is safe, he finds himself losing his heart to a woman whose faith and determination challenge him to look for God in the smallest of things and in the worst of circumstances.

I hope you enjoy Lark and Cyrus's adventures in this third installment of the Mission: Rescue series.

Blessings!

Shirlee McCoy